RE

What bothered
willing and read
one wanted to
ten to a radio show about horses. Maybe we just need
more publicity for *Horse Talk,* so that legitimate callers
phone in."

"I was thinking more along the lines of posting
Chad's naked baby pictures all over Fenton Hall,"
Stevie said. "Or maybe we could come up with some
good reason for blackmail."

"Why don't we try talking to Chad?" Lisa suggested.
"Maybe if we appeal to his better side—tell him how
important this is to us—he'll knock it off."

He doesn't have a better side," Stevie growled.

"Yeah," Carole said. "I mean, he might have a better
side, but from what we've seen of Chad before, telling
him how important *Horse Talk* is to us will just inspire
him to bother us more. Maybe if we leave him alone,
he'll leave us alone, too."

"I wouldn't count on that," Stevie said. "Revenge is
the best option. But, like you said, we've got all week."

THE SADDLE CLUB

HORSE TALK

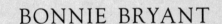

BONNIE BRYANT

A SKYLARK BOOK
NEW YORK • TORONTO • LONDON • SYDNEY • AUCKLAND

RL 5, 009–012

HORSE TALK

A Bantam Skylark Book / November 1997

ISBN 0-553-48426-5

Published simultaneously in the United States and Canada.

PRINTED IN THE UNITED STATES OF AMERICA

OPM   0 9 8 7 6 5 4 3 2 1

I would like to express my special thanks to Kimberly Brubaker Bradley for her help in the writing of this book.

"OKAY, RIDERS, THAT'S enough. Class is dismissed. Good work, everybody." Max Regnery, owner of Pine Hollow Stables, spoke quietly, but the half dozen riders in the ring responded immediately and gladly, sitting back and bringing their sweating horses to a walk. Stevie Lake blew out her breath and let her shoulders sag. That had been tough! For the past few minutes, Max had made them all canter with their feet out of the stirrups and one hand held straight up over their heads. He said it would improve their seats in the saddle. Riding without stirrups was fun, but it was hard work, and even though the November breeze was cool, Stevie, like her horse, Belle, was starting to sweat. She put her feet back into her stirrups and let her leg muscles relax.

1

Stevie patted Belle on the neck and turned her toward the gate. One of Stevie's best friends, Lisa Atwood, rode up to her on a mare named Prancer. "Wasn't that fun!" Lisa said. Her face was glowing from excitement and exercise. "We rode almost the whole lesson without stirrups! I've never done that before."

Stevie grinned back. "It was fun—but hard. I had a long day at school, too, and I'm tired."

"I know," Lisa said. "We missed talking to you before the lesson." On Tuesdays after school, the girls and their other best friend, Carole Hanson, had riding lessons. Stevie had come in late that day and had barely had time to saddle Belle before the lesson started.

"Let's walk out on the trails for a few minutes," Stevie suggested. "Carole!" She waved to their friend, who was sitting on her horse, Starlight, in the center of the ring and talking earnestly to Max. "Look at her," Stevie said. "You can tell by the way she's waving her hands that she's explaining some complicated riding theory to Max."

"Maybe," Lisa said. Carole was a fantastic rider, the best of the three of them (she planned to be a professional horse something—vet, rider, trainer—someday), and Starlight was a great horse, but they hadn't had one of their better lessons. Lisa could tell by watching them jump that they had never been quite in harmony the entire hour. She hoped Carole wasn't upset.

"Yeah," Stevie said sympathetically, catching Lisa's meaning. "Well, a nice little trail ride will cheer her up, too. Carole! Come on! We're going to take a loop through the woods."

Carole said one last thing to Max and turned toward them. She was smiling; she didn't look, Lisa thought, too upset about the lesson. "Great idea," Carole said as she rode up to her friends. "These horses are going to take a while to cool down anyway, and that way we can relax without Mrs. Reg finding eight hundred things for us to do."

Lisa laughed. Mrs. Reg, Max's mother, ran the stables, and she was notorious for setting idle hands to work.

The horses were all sweating under their thick winter coats, and the girls had to make sure they were absolutely dry before they put them back into their stalls; otherwise the horses could get sick. Riding them at a walk was actually a pretty good way to cool them. "We'll make sure they're really, really cool," Lisa said. "We'll probably have to take a very long ride."

Stevie told Max where they were going. "Be back before it gets dark," he warned them, then waved them off with a smile.

"He's so nice to us," Lisa said appreciatively. Unlike

3

her friends, she didn't have her own horse. Prancer, the mare she was riding, belonged to Max. Lisa loved Prancer very much, and Max usually let her take her out for trail rides and other fun things, as well as ride her in lessons.

"You sure had a great lesson, Lisa," Carole told her as they rode down the short path that led into the woods.

"Thanks," Lisa said with a grin. She knew it was true. Today they'd jumped fences without stirrups and without holding on to their reins; to Lisa, who'd never done anything like it before, it had felt wonderfully free, like flying. She loved to learn; she was a straight-A student in school, and she studied lots of other things like dance, piano, and acting. Horses were her favorite subject, but she hadn't been riding as long as her two friends, and when she had started she had been somewhat surprised at how much there was to learn. Horses couldn't be figured out by reading a book. They had minds of their own.

"You were the star of The Saddle Club," Stevie complimented her. "Belle and I weren't quite as together as you and Prancer."

Long ago, the three of them had decided that they loved horses enough to form The Saddle Club. Its only two rules were that members had to be horse-crazy, and they had to help each other out.

"You looked great except for that bounce combination," Lisa replied. A bounce combination was two fences set so close together that the horse jumped one, landed, and immediately jumped the other without taking another stride. Belle had insisted on taking a stride between the fences, and Stevie, riding without reins or stirrups, had come awfully close to falling off.

Stevie shook her head. "I don't know what got into Belle," she said. "She's done bounces dozens of times." She shrugged. "Oh well. We got it right in the end."

Lisa and Carole smiled at her. Stevie was a good rider, too, particularly at a kind of elegant flat work called dressage. Belle was good at both dressage and jumping, and she loved to be taken out on trail rides; she seemed to enjoy having a good time as much as Stevie did. But while Stevie never cared how well she did in school (except, of course, when her low grades meant her parents wouldn't let her ride), she was very competitive in the saddle. Sometimes she lost patience with herself, or with Belle, when things didn't go right.

"Don't look so proud of me," she said to her friends. "It's not like our riding lesson was any big deal."

"It's not like Phil was there," Lisa teased. Phil Marsten was Stevie's boyfriend, and he rode, too.

"I could tell Belle just wasn't getting it," Stevie explained. "She wasn't understanding what we wanted her to do. It wasn't like she was trying to be bad."

"Exactly," Carole said with a nod. "I felt the same way about Starlight. We— Hey!" She exclaimed as

Starlight jumped sideways in alarm. They had ridden out of the woods for a moment and were about to cross a small hay field. An old tractor was parked in the corner of the field, and Starlight reacted as if it were a monster. Every muscle in his sleek body tensed.

"Come on, boy, nothing to be afraid of," Carole said soothingly. "It's just a tractor. It's not going to hurt you." They had to walk past the tractor to get back onto the trail.

Starlight refused to walk forward. He bunched his hindquarters beneath him, and when Carole gently pushed him forward with her legs, he tossed his head and tried to turn in circles. "No," Carole said firmly but calmly. "Walk on."

"We'll give you a lead," Stevie offered. She rode Belle past the tractor and turned her to face Starlight. Starlight rolled his eyes and tossed his head again. Carole continued to urge him forward, and he continued to resist her urgings. Prancer, worried that Starlight might have something to be afraid of, refused to join Belle on the far side of the tractor, but she didn't fight Lisa the way Starlight was fighting Carole.

"Come on. Come on," Carole said persistently. She pushed Starlight forward with her legs and seat. Starlight took one hesitant step, then another.

"You've got him," Stevie said encouragingly.

Starlight took one more step, then whirled, bucked, and bolted for safety. Carole landed on the grass on her backside. Before Stevie or Lisa could dismount to help her, she was standing up and laughing.

"Are you okay?" Stevie asked with concern. They all fell off sometimes—all riders did—and it was never a particularly pleasant experience.

"I'm fine," Carole assured them. "Look. The grass is so thick it's like carpet."

"I'm so sorry," Lisa said. "You're having a tough day."

"Well," Carole said, laughing again, "at least it's consistent. Yet another case of not listening to my horse!"

The others laughed as well. In the middle of the lesson, when Carole had been struggling to anticipate Starlight's jumps, Max had finally cried in exasperation, "Carole, you've got to listen to your horse!"

"But Max," Stevie had piped up sweetly from across the ring, "you always say horses don't understand English, and I don't think Carole speaks anything else."

Everyone had laughed. "I can count to ten in Spanish," Carole had offered. "Should I try that?"

Max had grinned and replied, "No, I think you should all learn to speak horse."

"Hang on just a second," Carole said now. She wiped some wisps of dried grass off her breeches, then walked slowly to the corner of the field where Starlight stood waiting. In another moment she was mounted.

This time, Stevie and Lisa walked their horses quietly past the tractor and then waited on the other side. Carole let Starlight take a long look at the frightening object, then asked him to walk forward as she had before. Starlight did. "Good boy," Carole said, patting him.

"You're really in a good mood," Stevie told her. "I mean, you don't seem upset about falling off or about that lesson. I know you weren't riding horribly, but you weren't riding your best, either."

"I'm just not worried about it," Carole answered. "I mean, I can't have a great lesson every week. And in a way it was kind of interesting—I don't even know why I felt so out of rhythm. Until I know, there's not much point in being upset."

Carole really meant what she said. Every single thing about horses fascinated her, and Max had told her once that you could learn just as much from a bad lesson as a good one, if you tried.

"And that fall was just silly," she continued. "I should have been ready for Starlight to whirl like that, and I probably should have let him take a really good look at the tractor before I tried to make him go past it. I could tell by how rigid his muscles were that he was upset." She laughed. "Maybe that's what Max meant by learning to speak horse. Maybe he meant learning to listen to their body cues."

Stevie thought about this. "I assumed he was joking, but you could be right," she said. "Belle pricks her ears forward when she sees me, and I always take that to mean hello."

"And we tell them what to do with our hands and legs," Lisa added. "It's kind of cool when you think about it. It's horse talk—a whole other kind of communication."

"Our school's on a huge communication theme right now," Carole told Stevie. She and Lisa went to the same public school, while Stevie attended a private school, Fenton Hall.

"That's right," Lisa cut in. "We didn't have time to tell you our news before the lesson, Stevie."

"Everybody's studying television, newspapers, the Internet, and things like African drum signals, Egyptian hieroglyphs, Chinese characters, sign language, and Braille," Carole said. "Best of all—"

"We're going to have a radio show!" said Lisa.

"Wow!" Stevie was impressed. "Just the two of you?"

Carole and Lisa looked at each other. "We haven't had a chance to discuss that yet," Lisa admitted. "Maybe, but I kind of doubt we'll be allowed to. It would be fun, though."

"I think so, too," Carole agreed. She checked her watch and signaled to them that it was time to turn for home. Lisa ran her hand down Prancer's shoulder. The mare was cool and dry.

"See," Carole explained, "the local radio station offered to do an educational cooperative with us. Every day for the entire month, our school gets an hour of radio time. The station is loaning us equipment and is going to teach us how to use it. We have to come up with programs to fill all the airtime. Some students are going to be DJs, and others will do technical stuff, maybe even advertising—I don't really know yet. They announced it this morning, and tomorrow after school they're having a meeting for everyone who wants to take part. The airtime will be from four to five P.M., so it's an extracurricular activity. It's not a requirement."

"It really sounds fun," Stevie said enviously. "We don't do anything like that at Fenton. The last time we were on the radio was when Herbie Brewster set the chemistry lab on fire and we had to evacuate the building. Are you two going to do it?"

Carole and Lisa grinned at each other. "I think so, yes," Lisa said, "if it's okay that we're in different grades. What do you say?"

"I say yes," Carole replied. "I think we should try for one of the DJ positions. They'll be the most interesting. I know we'll make a great team."

"We already make a great team." Lisa let the reins slide through her fingers so that Prancer could stretch her neck. "That's what The Saddle Club is all about."

"So what kind of show will you have?" Stevie asked. "You'll have to have a theme."

"I don't know," Lisa said. "But I sure don't want to do another hour of the same old rock music. Every kid in my homeroom class wanted to do that."

"Mine too," Carole agreed. "We'll do something unique."

LISA TWISTED HER hair nervously around her finger. "I didn't think there'd be so many kids here," she whispered to Carole.

"Me either," Carole whispered back. They were waiting in the hallway outside the room that Mrs. Klemme, the radio program moderator, had set up as a studio. Three or four pairs of kids waited in front of them, and more had already gone inside. All the DJs were going to have to work in pairs, and each DJ pair had to present its idea for a show to Mrs. Klemme, one at a time.

"Well," Lisa said, brightening a little, "I think we're well prepared to present our idea. I've got the playlist right here." She patted her notebook confidently.

They had decided to do a music show after all, and

the night before they'd pooled all their most recent tapes and come up with a list of their favorite songs. A music show would be easy, and it would also be a lot of fun—not only would they get to talk on the air, but they'd also be listening to what they wanted to hear!

Two boys came out of Mrs. Klemme's room, scowling. "Guess she didn't like their idea," Carole said, nudging Lisa with her elbow and nodding toward the boys.

"Guess not." Lisa frowned. "Weren't they planning on doing a music show, like us?"

"Ours will be much better," Carole assured her. Lisa nodded.

But the next two pairs of kids went in and out of Mrs. Klemme's room so quickly that Lisa thought it looked as if they were using a revolving door. She grabbed a girl from the second pair. "What's wrong?" Lisa asked. "Why isn't she listening to anyone's ideas?"

The girl, whom Lisa knew slightly from class, rolled her eyes in disgust. "She says she's not taking any more music shows. She's got enough scheduled already, she says." The girl sounded peeved. "She wouldn't even look at our playlist!"

"Uh-oh." Lisa and Carole looked at each other in dismay. "That's what we were going to do, too."

"Better change your minds fast, or give up being a DJ," the girl advised as she walked away.

"Wow," Carole said. "What should we do?"

13

"We have to think of something quick," Lisa said. "How about a talk show?"

Carole shook her head, laughing. "The only thing *I* know enough to talk about is horses. Who's going to listen to that?"

"I don't know," Lisa said. She tried to come up with a better idea, but the door opened and it was their turn.

"Horse Talk!" Carole said to Mrs. Klemme. "We thought we'd do a talk show called *Horse Talk.* About horses."

Mrs. Klemme looked pleased. "That's a different idea," she said. "A call-in show, you mean?"

"Uh . . . sure," Lisa said. "Like the gardening show my mom listens to. People call in and ask questions about how to take care of gardenias and stuff, only they'll be asking us how to take care of horses."

"All about horses," Carole corrected her. "Not just how to care for them. Anything people want to ask, we'll answer."

Mrs. Klemme smiled. "It's a relief to hear from a pair who don't want to do another music show! I don't know anything about horses myself. I assume you two do?"

They nodded. "We've been riding for years," Carole said.

"Horse Talk it is," Ms. Klemme said, adding the title to her chart. "You'll be on the air a week from today."

Lisa and Carole looked at one another. What had they gotten themselves into?

"A TALK SHOW about horses? Here?" Max looked amused and a little skeptical. "Where did you get that idea?" Lisa and Carole had come straight from the meeting to the stables. They'd had time to tell Stevie all about their plans before Max had finished a lesson he was teaching. Stevie thought *Horse Talk* was a fabulous idea. She couldn't wait to help out.

"Come on, Max," Lisa pleaded. "It was the best idea we could think of. We're the only call-in show. And we already told Mrs. Klemme we could probably have it here."

"Live from Pine Hollow," Carole told him. "It's exciting. It's authentic."

"It's publicity," Stevie pointed out. "This could make Pine Hollow famous—really put it on the map. You'll probably get a bunch of new students because of *Horse Talk*."

Max grinned. "Only if Lisa and Carole answer the questions correctly," he said.

"Max!" Lisa protested. "You know we know more about horses than most people who listen to the radio." Lisa knew that no one knew everything about riding, but she also knew that many people didn't know anything at all.

"Between Lisa's acting ability and Carole's incredible wealth of knowledge, how can they go wrong?" Stevie asked. She smiled at Max. "Plus, they'll have my behind-the-scenes help. It'll be a certain success— if you say we can do it."

"If anyone can make a horse chat show a success, I believe you three could," Max said. "You certainly talk about horses enough. I guess you can hold it here."

"Thanks!" Lisa said. "Mrs. Klemme said she'd stop by later in the week to discuss the details with you. Max, you won't regret this."

"I'm sure I won't," he replied.

Stevie squeezed Lisa's arm excitedly. "This is the best Saddle Club project ever!"

LISA AND CAROLE spent the next couple of days getting ready for *Horse Talk*. On Thursday they learned how to set up and operate the portable equipment that would let them broadcast from Pine Hollow. On Friday morning they met with some of the students who were doing behind-the-scenes work for the project. They picked out music for a theme song and learned how to play the prerecorded advertising tapes.

"Phew!" Lisa said as they walked into the stable together on Saturday morning. "All the radio stuff has been fun, but I'm glad we'll be riding today!"

"You and me both," Carole replied. "Max said we could tell everyone about *Horse Talk* at Horse Wise

16

today." Horse Wise was the Pony Club that most of the kids at Pine Hollow belonged to. It helped them learn all sorts of things about horses, and it met almost every Saturday morning. Today they were having a brief meeting in the office, and then a session on horseback.

They hung their coats in their cubbies in the locker room. Stevie appeared shortly, and the three of them headed for the meeting. Most of the other Pony Clubbers were already inside. Max spent the first few minutes of the meeting discussing some changes in the schedule for the next month. Then he asked Lisa to tell everyone about *Horse Talk*.

"It's new, it's exciting, and it's live from Pine Hollow!" Lisa began. Her acting classes had taught her the importance of an energetic opening line, but this one fizzled: The Pony Clubbers looked blank. "*Horse Talk* is a radio show Carole and I will be broadcasting from Pine Hollow—live every Wednesday afternoon!" she said. She explained her school's project. "So if any of you have horse questions you want answered, you know where to call! And if you just like to hear about horses, tune in every Wednesday, live from Pine Hollow!" Despite the enthusiasm Lisa tried to put into her voice, no one looked very excited.

"What a splendid idea," Veronica diAngelo drawled, her sarcastic tone making the idea seem not splendid but hopelessly stupid. Veronica was one of the most annoying riders in the barn. "What kind of school do you go to, where they teach you things like that?" she asked. Veronica went to Fenton Hall, the same as Stevie, and she knew perfectly well where Lisa, Carole, and most of the other kids went to school.

Lisa flushed but decided to ignore Veronica. "It'll be great," she promised the group. "Just tune in and see. Any questions?" To Lisa's relief, May Grover raised her hand. "Yes, May?" Lisa asked the younger girl.

"Why would we want to call you on the phone to ask you a question when we can just ask you in person?" May demanded. "Especially when you're already at the stable."

"Well—"

"Or we could just ask Max," May's friend Jasmine James cut in. "He knows more than you guys, even, and he's usually around."

"Because it'll be fun," Stevie said. "You'll get to hear your voice on the radio. All your friends will hear you."

"Not if they aren't listening," May said.

Lisa looked increasingly flustered, and Stevie felt exasperated. "So tell them to listen," Stevie told May. "Tell everyone you know. It'll be a great show!"

"Thank you, Lisa and Stevie," Max said. "Thank you, Carole."

Lisa sat down gratefully and exchanged annoyed

glances with Carole. How could the entire Pony Club be so shortsighted? *Horse Talk* was a fabulous idea.

"One more item on our agenda before we ride," Max said. "Janey, come on up here, please." He motioned to a small girl Carole had not noticed before. She was dressed in neat but not fussy riding clothes, and she had a Pony Club pin on the collar of her jacket. She looked about May's age, or maybe a little younger.

"This is Janey," Max said, turning her around to face the other kids. Janey didn't quite meet their eyes; Carole guessed she didn't feel comfortable in front of so many strangers. *Oh, well,* Carole thought. *No one is ever a stranger at Pine Hollow for long.*

"Janey is from New Zealand," Max continued. "Her parents are working in Washington, D.C., for a few months and living in Willow Creek, so Janey's going to ride with us while she's here. I want you all to make her welcome. Stevie, I want you to take special care of her. You'll be her big sister, okay?"

"Sure, Max," Stevie said cheerfully. Max often had them learn things in big sister–little sister pairs. She waved at Janey, but Janey just hung her head a little and didn't wave back. Stevie wondered why the girl looked so glum.

"If you have any problems or questions and you can't find me, you ask Stevie," Max told Janey. "And Stevie will help you tack your pony up for the lesson today, too."

19

Janey spoke so softly, her reply was hard to hear. She had a funny accent that was difficult for Stevie to understand. The Saddle Club had gone to a Pony Club competition in England, and Stevie had become accustomed to English accents, but Janey's was not quite the same.

"She'll be riding Nickel today," Max told Stevie. The rest of Horse Wise was already dispersing, but Lisa and Carole stayed with Stevie and introduced themselves to Janey. The little girl scarcely responded to them, only muttering, "Hello," before looking away. She wasn't very friendly.

"Come on," Stevie said gently, leading her down the aisle. "I'll show you the tack room and then I'll take you to Nickel. Do you know how to tack up? Shall I show you how?"

Janey's eyes widened. "I'm not *daft*," she said.

"I didn't say you were," Stevie said. She didn't understand Janey's reaction—she hadn't said anything to upset her. She was just trying to be helpful.

"I can tack up a horse," Janey said.

Stevie shrugged. "At some stables around here, the kids just get on and ride," she explained. "Some kids come to Pony Club and don't know how to tack up."

"In New Zealand we learn everything proper," Janey said with a fierce frown.

20

Stevie sighed. She had always liked having a little sister before, but this particular little sister didn't seem like much fun. She took Janey to the tack room and pointed out Nickel's saddle, bridle, and grooming equipment. Then she took her down the aisle to meet the pony. Nickel was a shaggy, extremely gentle gray pony. He was one of Stevie's favorites.

"Here he is," Stevie said grandly. She pulled a carrot out of her jacket pocket and broke off a piece for Nickel. He stuck his nose over the stall door and asked for more.

Janey dropped her saddle on the nearby rack with a thump. "I'm riding that lump?" she asked. "That's bloody! Am I going to be stuck on him the whole time?"

"He's a great pony. I don't know whether you'll *get to* ride him the whole time or not." Stevie put great emphasis on the words *get to*. Riding was a privilege, and Janey should feel fortunate that Max had assigned her a pony as nice as Nickel.

"He's not much like my Fancy, that's all," Janey said softly.

"He's fancy enough," Stevie retorted. She knew that some show ponies looked like miniature Thoroughbreds; she also knew that those cost about a zillion dollars and weren't likely to be used for lessons anywhere. She didn't know what Janey's problem was.

21

Janey made a noise that sounded like a growl. Stevie decided to ignore it. "You shouldn't thump your saddle around like that," she said instead. "Saddles have pieces of wood in the middle of them, and if you break the wood you've wrecked the saddle."

Janey's eyes widened again. "Really?" she said. "How about the bridle? Does it have wood in it, too?"

"Of course not," Stevie said. "Look—"

Janey let out a snort that was almost a laugh. "I was joking," she said. "I know about saddles. My instructor at home cut an old one in half so we could see the insides."

"Oh." Stevie felt a little foolish, and it annoyed her that a kid Janey's age was making her feel that way. "Well, look. We've got to hurry or Max will get mad, and I've got my own horse to get ready. If you know so much about saddles, you can tack Nickel up by yourself. Just go on out to the ring when you're done."

"Yes, miss," Janey said, softly and a little sadly.

Stevie wondered if Janey was being sarcastic again or if that was how people from New Zealand usually talked. She felt she wasn't being a very good big sister, but she didn't know what she should be doing differently. She was afraid she didn't actually like Janey very much. She shook her head and went to saddle Belle. Probably Janey just needed a little more time to adjust to Pine Hollow.

* * *

22

WHEN CAROLE RODE into the ring for the mounted portion of the Pony Club meeting, she had to laugh. She gave Starlight's neck a pat. "Look," she said, "it's our second chance." Max had set up the same type of gymnastic exercises that Carole had struggled over in Tuesday's lesson. Some of the fences were a little lower to accommodate the smaller ponies.

This time Carole got it right. She focused on feeling Starlight's body move, and she tried to let herself move with him. "Very good, Carole!" Max shouted the second time she rode down the line of jumps.

Carole grinned from ear to ear. She could feel that she was doing well. "I'm listening a little better today," she told him.

"That's right." To Carole's surprise, Max held up his hand and spoke to the entire group. "Carole is listening to her horse—not just with her ears, but with her legs and seat and hands. Everybody got that? That's what you want to try to do."

At the end of the session, Carole's friends rode up to congratulate her. "That was miles better," Lisa said. "You're back at the top of the class."

"Thanks." Carole beamed and gave Starlight another pat. "Did you guys see Janey? I couldn't watch her much because she was riding right behind me, but she looked really great."

"I couldn't ever really see her, either," Lisa admitted, "but Max sure said a lot of nice things to her."

"Um-hm," Stevie said noncommittally. She was embarrassed to admit that she hadn't really thought about or watched Janey at all.

"Hey, Janey!" Lisa waved her crop to attract the little girl's attention. "You did great!"

Janey scowled. "I don't need your sarcasm," she retorted. She turned Nickel away from them, hitched up the back of her trousers, and stalked away.

"But I wasn't being sarcastic," Lisa said softly. She turned to Carole. "Why would she think I was?"

Carole shrugged. "Did we miss something? Maybe she made some mistakes we didn't see."

"She doesn't have to be rude about it," Lisa said.

"I bet she's still in a tiff about riding Nickel," Stevie said. "She told me he wasn't fancy enough for her."

"Really!" Carole was disgusted. "He's fancy enough for us. I hope Janey's not another Veronica diAngelo."

WHILE THEY WERE putting their horses away, Mrs. Klemme came into the stable. Lisa pointed her in the direction of Max's office, and after a few minutes she came back out, waved to Lisa and Carole, and drove away. A few minutes later, Max came down the aisle.

"Turns out your radio project needs a lot of space and a few electrical outlets," he said in a dry tone.

"Yeah," Lisa said, nodding. She remembered the big binder full of radio project information she'd been given. They would need a lot of equipment to do their show.

"Turns out there's only one place in the stable that's big enough," Max said. He sounded annoyed, but there was a glimmer of a smile around the edges of his mouth.

"What place is that?" Carole asked.

"In the stall row, right outside the tack room. It was there or the indoor ring, but the ring doesn't have outlets. Trust you three to end up in the middle of everything!" He turned and stalked away.

"Sorry," Lisa said. Stevie and Carole laughed.

Max turned back and smiled at them. "You're going to be live from Pine Hollow, all right. Wednesdays only—remember that. By Thursday morning I want my space back!"

"READY?" CAROLE SLID into her chair and pulled it close to the big folding table they'd set up. She put on her headphones. Her heart was thudding from excitement. In just a few moments they would be on the air!

"Ready!" Lisa took her place in another chair. The two friends grinned at one another. Lisa felt the quick thrill of nervousness that always went through her just as she was about to perform.

Stevie adjusted the stack of horse reference books Carole had put on the table. Lisa fiddled with one of the equipment controls. Carole cleared her throat noisily, and all three of them watched the second hand on the big stable wall clock slowly sweep around. In exactly half a minute, *Horse Talk* would premiere.

Stevie stood in front of the table, her eyes still on

the clock. She counted off the last few seconds—"Three! Two! One!"—for her friends, then sat down in the third chair to watch the show.

Exactly on cue, Lisa hit the button that put them on the air. Carole ran the tape that played their theme music—a classical piece that sounded a little like horses galloping—and Lisa read out their cleverly written introduction. ". . . We're coming to you live from Pine Hollow, Willow Creek's finest riding academy, every Wednesday for the next four weeks," she concluded. "*Horse Talk*. The phone number is 555–8151. That's 555–8151."

That was the stable phone number. It really wasn't worth the extra bother for them to get a special number just for *Horse Talk*, so they'd run a long extension phone line from the office. Mrs. Reg had not been too happy about having her phone tied up for an hour every week, but she had let them use it after they'd promised to repay her by spending an extra hour each week cleaning stalls.

Lisa licked her dry lips and smiled encouragingly at Carole. Carole nodded and spoke into the microphone. "I'm Carole Hanson. I'm a C-3 level Pony Club member, and I own a horse named Starlight. Lisa and I are pleased to take your calls. 555–8151."

There was a short pause while they looked at one another. By now the phone was supposed to have rung. They weren't supposed to air their first commercial for seven more minutes. "That's 555–8151," Lisa repeated. "And, uh, I'm Lisa Atwood, and, uh—" Mrs. Klemme had told them and told them not to say *uh*. Lisa felt herself blushing. She was glad she was on the radio, where no one could see.

"We're *Horse Talk,* live from Pine Hollow!" Carole cut in. Lisa gave her a grateful look. It wasn't the most fabulous statement in the world, but it gave Lisa a chance to recover. No matter what, Mrs. Klemme had told them, they were to avoid broadcasting silence. That was called dead air, and it was the worst thing that could happen in radio. You always had to give people something to listen to.

"And our number is 555–8151. We're waiting to take your calls," Lisa said. The phone was still dead. Lisa wondered if somehow they'd managed to unplug it by mistake. She gestured to Stevie to check the cord. "Maybe we should tell our listeners a little about ourselves, Carole. How long have you been riding?"

Carole gave a little laugh that came out as a squeak. She rolled her eyes in agony. "Well, I can't really remember when I started taking lessons," she said. "My mother rode, and my father is in the Marine Corps, and there are usually stables on base. I guess you could say I grew up with horses."

Stevie gestured to show that the phone was plugged in. She picked up the receiver and checked for a dial tone. "Put it down," Carole whispered fiercely. "What if someone finally called in and got a busy signal?"

"I'm the opposite of Carole," Lisa said into the microphone. "I started riding rather late in life, and I've only been doing it for a few years. I guess I'm proof that you don't have to grow up with horses to love them. Here at Pine Hollow Stables, the owner, Max Regnery, even teaches adult beginners to ride."

"There are really no age restrictions," Carole said. "We'll take calls from people of any age, too. Remember, our number is 555–8151." She slapped her forehead. Boy, did that sound dumb!

Lisa started to say something, but her mind locked up. "Uhhh—"

"Commercial break!" Carole blurted. She hit the button that started the first advertising tape. All three girls sighed in relief. They had two minutes to talk to each other off the air before the ads were done.

"That was only four and a half minutes!" Lisa said.

"I know," Carole groaned. "I ran the ad too early, but I couldn't think of anything else to say."

"I was sure stuck," Lisa said. "I thought this would be easy, and all I can manage to say is *uh*! What are we going to do for an hour?"

Carole shook her head.

"The time will go faster once you start answering questions," Stevie said soothingly.

"We need questions," Carole said. "Stevie, do something. Find someone to call in."

"I will," Stevie promised. She slipped down the aisle.

Lisa looked at the clock. They had forty-five seconds left before the ad tape finished. "What are we going to say?"

"Well," Carole suggested, "maybe you could ask me about Starlight. Then we could talk about how to choose a horse. After that—I don't know, maybe you could explain the colors of horses or something like that."

The colors of horses! Lisa shook her head. "I hope we don't get that desperate," she said. But she couldn't think of a better topic. She hoped the phone would ring.

"Stevie will do something," Carole said comfortingly as the tape finished and *Horse Talk* went back on the air.

STEVIE HURRIED THROUGH the stable. On Wednesdays, Max taught many of the younger riders. Their lesson had ended at four o'clock, so they were all still in the stable taking care of their horses.

"Hi, Stevie!" Jessica Adler said. "Why aren't you listening to Carole and Lisa? Max said he was going to try to find a radio." Jessica smiled at Stevie, and Stevie smiled back. Stevie really liked the little girl. When

Jessica had first come to Pine Hollow, she had been shy and very lonely, but she'd warmed up to The Saddle Club right away.

"They need callers," Stevie explained. "Call in and ask a question, okay?"

Jessica frowned. "But they're using the phone. I don't have anywhere to call from."

"Use the pay phone."

"I don't have a quarter."

Stevie frowned. Neither did she. "Well, come with me and we'll figure something out."

Jessica looked sorry. "I can't, I have to leave early—" A car horn honked outside.

"That's okay, go," Stevie said. "I'll find someone else."

"I'll do it next time!" Jessica ran out of the stable.

Jessica's shout reverberated through the stable. Lisa flinched. The car horn had been broadcast, too. She was beginning to understand the dangers of using a remote location. Why hadn't they chosen the school's quiet sound station? Any minute now, some kid was going to barge in, shouting that they needed something from the tack room. "So, Carole," Lisa said, "perhaps we should advise our listeners as to how to choose a horse."

"Good question, Lisa," Carole said. "The first consideration, of course . . ."

* * *

31

"C'MON, MAY," STEVIE urged. "Do it for Carole."

"I haven't got any questions," May said. "I'll come up with some by next week, I promise."

"If there is a next week," Stevie muttered. *Horse Talk!* She wondered what Carole and Lisa were talking about.

Stevie spied Janey cleaning out Nickel's water bucket. "Perfect!" she said. She went into the stall and grabbed Janey by the arm. "C'mon, I need your help," she said as she pulled Janey out and latched the door. "You're my little sister, so you can't say no."

Janey didn't seem unwilling. "Where are we going?"

"To Max and Deborah's house. I need you to help me make a phone call."

To Stevie's surprise, Janey grinned. "Okay. Who're we calling?"

"Lisa and Carole. It's for their radio show. You know, *Horse Talk*." Stevie didn't elaborate. Everyone at Pine Hollow knew about the radio show. She ran up the steps of Max's house with Janey close on her heels. There was a phone in the living room, right off the front hall. Stevie dialed the office phone number and thrust the receiver at Janey. "Here you go."

"Hi, Lisa!" Janey said brightly. "Hi, Carole! Are you guys having fun? I wanted to look for something in the tack room, but Max said you were busy."

Inside the stable, Lisa gulped in horror. They had

the phone hooked straight up to their equipment, so Janey's casual comment was broadcast to the world. "H-Hello, caller," Lisa stammered, in what she hoped was a very professional tone. "How may we help you?"

Inside Max's living room, Stevie grabbed Janey's shoulder and shook it. "You're not supposed to know them," she whispered.

Janey looked confused. "But I do know them," she said. She still held the receiver next to her chin, and Stevie knew that the radio audience could hear every word.

"Ask them a question," she whispered.

"But I don't have a question," Janey whispered back.

Finally, Lisa figured out how to handle Janey's call: She hung up the phone. "Whoops, we got cut off," she said cheerfully. "Remember, we're *Horse Talk*, and our phone number is 555–8151."

Janey rubbed her shoulder where Stevie had grabbed her. "They hung up," she said, sounding hurt.

Stevie took the phone away from her. "It's a good thing!" she said. "Why did you act like you knew them? This is supposed to be a radio show! You're supposed to be asking them for advice!"

Janey drew her eyebrows together and pushed out her lower lip. "You didn't tell me," she said. "You said, 'Help me make a phone call,' and I did." She turned and stalked out of Max's house.

Stevie sighed in exasperation. Nothing was going right. With a growing sense of desperation, she picked up the phone and redialed.

Brrrrnng! Carole's and Lisa's hands collided in the air over the Answer button. "Another question!" Lisa chirped, gesturing for Carole to answer it. "I guess we'll resume our discussion about the colors of horses some other time."

"Horse Talk!" Carole said. "How may we help you?"

"Uhhh . . . ," the caller said. "Um, could you tell me what color a palomino is?"

Carole looked at Lisa, who nodded. They'd heard that voice on their phones at home a hundred times in the past three months alone. It was Stevie. And Stevie must not be anywhere near a radio, because Carole had actually just discussed palomino horses thirty seconds before.

"Okay," Carole said, trying hard to sound cheerful and helpful, "I'll go over that again. A palomino is a golden-haired horse. A blond."

"Thank you," Stevie said, and hung up. Carole hit the button to hang up, but she wished Stevie had stayed on the line. What would they talk about now?

"We're *Horse Talk*," Lisa said. "555–8151." The phone rang again, and Lisa jabbed the button in relief.

"Hi," said the caller. It was Stevie again. "I take riding lessons, and I'm having a little trouble when I jump fences. My body comes too far out of the saddle. Any advice?"

"Sure," Carole said. "You could try gymnastic exercises."

"Remember to wait for the horse," Lisa added. "Let him jump; don't try to jump the fence for him."

"Thanks," Stevie said. Lisa hung up. The phone rang again immediately, and it was Stevie asking whether polo wraps or shin boots were better protection for open jumpers.

That was the way the rest of the show went. After every call, Lisa hung up, the phone rang again immediately, and it was always Stevie. At some point she must have found a Pony Club manual in Max and Deborah's living room, because the questions she asked became more like a Pony Club examination: "What are the four natural aids?" "When you are jumping, should your stirrups be longer or shorter than when you are not?" "How often do horses require vaccinations?" Fortunately, all this was material Carole could rattle off with ease. Unfortunately, every question and answer took less than a minute, so Stevie had to come up with a lot of questions.

The minute hand on the clock slowly dragged its way back to the top of the hour. Lisa felt as though all her life force had been drained from her. Every time the phone rang, she hoped that it would finally be a real, non-Stevie question, and every time she heard Stevie's voice her hopes were cruelly dashed. It wasn't Stevie's fault—what would they have done without her? They would have ended up with the deadest of dead air, broken only by Lisa saying, "Uh."

Worst of all, thought Lisa, *Horse Talk* was boring. It had to be obvious to anyone who was listening for very long that all the questions were coming from one person. And if it was that obvious, no one was going to listen very long.

The hour felt like a week, but finally it came to an end. Lisa managed a semicheerful, "See you next week at the same time, from the same place, beautiful Pine Hollow Stables. We're *Horse Talk*!" Carole pushed the button that started their exit music before they both collapsed across the table.

"I can't move," Carole muttered. "I think I'll just lie here until next week. After all the questions I answered, I ought to be a B-rated Pony Clubber by now, at least."

"Uh-huh," agreed Lisa. It felt so good to be able to say "uh" without panicking that she said it a few more times. "Uh. Uh. Uhhh."

"*Uh* or *ugh*?" Stevie asked. She came in and threw herself dramatically across the floor. "Not that I mind—I'd do anything for you guys—but my fingers are practically bleeding from dialing 555–8151 that

36

many times. Why can't Max join the twentieth century and get speed dial on his phone?"

"Don't know," said Lisa. She started to lift her head to look at Stevie, but it was too much effort, so she put her head back down.

"You know what's really awful?" Carole asked without moving. "We have to do this three more times."

"Ugh," said Lisa. "Definitely ugh."

"YOU WON'T BELIEVE what Mrs. Klemme said to me in the hall today," Carole told Lisa and Stevie with a groan. It was Friday night, and The Saddle Club was having a sleepover at Stevie's house. The girls were making plans for the next *Horse Talk*.

"What?" asked Stevie. "She's the radio program moderator, right?"

Carole nodded. "After apologizing for not being with us for the broadcast, she said we did a great job and obviously didn't need her! She said that we spoke clearly and slowly, and we seemed comfortable on the air—"

"She must not have listened to the beginning," Lisa muttered.

"—but she was surprised by how technical the call-in questions were," Carole continued. "She said we should try to encourage more general questions, too."

Lisa snorted. "Did she suggest any ways to encourage more *questioners?* That seemed to be our problem."

Carole shook her head. "I'm not sure she realized that it was just one person calling in."

Lisa shrugged. She was trying hard not to feel bitter about the whole radio program. *Horse Talk* had been her idea, and she liked to be successful in everything. So far she couldn't count *Horse Talk* a success, and she didn't have much hope for its improving. "Mrs. Klemme told me she was impressed with how much you and I knew about horses," she told Carole.

"Most people don't know much at all," Stevie commented. She stuck her head under her bed and retrieved a few horse books that were gathering dust there. "I mean, no one else in our families has any clue. Most of the kids at school don't ride. Even a lot of people who like horses don't get the chance to learn much about them. When you think about it, *Horse Talk* is a public service."

"Two people have told me they were listening," Lisa said. "Two. That's all."

"I think Max found a radio by the end," Carole said.

"Anyway," Lisa said, forcing a smile because she didn't want to inflict her bad mood on her friends, "this week we'll be prepared to not get questions. Is that all your books, Stevie?"

"Yep." Stevie added the ones from underneath the bed to a waist-high pile beside the bed. "Except for fiction, of course."

Lisa emptied her backpack. "I didn't bring the ones that I knew you already had."

Carole patted a bulging duffel bag. "I brought as many of mine as I could. They wouldn't all fit." Lisa and Stevie laughed. No wonder Carole knew so much about horses! She must have had ten books on jumping alone.

The Saddle Club had faced up to the fact that they might not get real callers for *Horse Talk*. The best way to be prepared, they had decided, was to make a list of good questions that Stevie could ask. That way they would always have something interesting, or at least relevant, to say. They were going to read through all their horse books for ideas.

"I was talking to my mom about the gardening show she listens to," Lisa said as she sharpened her pencil and took a fresh pad of paper out of her bag. "She says that the master gardener usually doesn't answer more than about fifteen questions per show."

"Fifteen!" Stevie exclaimed. "I asked at least fifty!"

"Right," Lisa said. "See, Mom says that the gardener talks to each caller for a while. He asks for details about their problem, and he discusses his solution, and they chitchat. Sometimes they make little jokes. And the gardener always talks to his callers by name. 'Well,

Jeremy, it sounds to me like your philodendron has an advanced case of root rot.' Like that."

"By name!" Stevie rolled her eyes in mock horror. "That'll work great for my *first* phone call. After that it'll be"—she dropped her voice in a bad imitation of Max—" 'Oh, here's Stevie again! Doesn't Stevie know anything about horses? Why does Stevie keep calling?' "

Carole tapped her cheek with her fingers. "We could make up names to go with the questions. It's a pretty good idea, really," she said. "If we take longer to answer each question, then we won't need to ask as many. It'll be easier."

"Plus, it'll sound more professional," Lisa said. "If we chat with our callers, and they all have different names, then no one will guess that they're really all Stevie."

"I guess I could try to disguise my voice," Stevie said.

"Sure," Lisa said. "It'll be easy. All it takes is a little practice."

Someone banged on Stevie's bedroom door. "Knock it off, Chad!" Stevie yelled without getting up. Stevie had three brothers, one older, one younger, and one twin. Chad, the oldest, was the only one who constantly bugged her.

Chad stuck his head in the door. "Mom says to tell you it's time for dinner."

Stevie and her friends got up. "Why didn't you say so right away, instead of knocking holes through my door?" Stevie groused. Chad sneered at her and ran down the stairs.

"Think of names," Lisa said. "We'll make a list after dinner."

"Oh, I'm thinking of names, all right," Stevie muttered, glaring at her brother's disappearing back. "They just aren't names I can use on the air."

"MARILLA," LISA SAID, writing it down. "I like that one."

"From *Anne of Green Gables?*" Stevie asked. "She was kind of a crabby old housewife, wasn't she? Let's see, Marilla can say, 'I don't understand why horses have to wear shoes on their feet. Can you explain it to me?' " Stevie's Marilla voice was high and a little strained.

"Great," said Carole. "That's a good question, too, because it'll take a long time to answer. You want to avoid yes-no questions, and try to ask ones that we can discuss on the air for a while."

"Do you think you could imitate a boy's voice?" Lisa asked. Stevie had gone through several characters, but so far they had all been female.

Stevie wrinkled up her face, thinking. "Maybe. A young boy's, anyway. And I could probably make my voice squeak, like Chad's." They laughed. Chad's voice

42

was starting to change. At dinner he'd asked Lisa to please pass the rolls. The *please* had started out very low and ended in a squeak that hurt their ears. Chad had looked awfully embarrassed.

"Why do people ride horses, anyway?" Stevie asked in a rude and hysterically funny imitation of Chad.

"That's easy," Carole said in a deep radio announcer's voice. She grabbed a hairbrush to use as a microphone. "Cats are too small, sloths are too slow, and giraffes are too big."

"And what about the smell?" Stevie continued, still pretending to be Chad.

"I admit it bothers us a little," Carole said into the hairbrush, "but don't worry, Chad, I don't think the horses will mind." Carole and Lisa shrieked with laughter.

Stevie grinned. "Here's another—see if you can guess who this is. *Actshually, I dain't laike Paine Haullow.*"

Lisa shook her head. "I understand the words, but sorry, I haven't got a clue who you're trying to be."

"Oh, come on!" Stevie said. "It's Janey! Who else?"

"I guess," Lisa said. "I haven't really talked to her much, but I don't have a hard time understanding her. I don't think her accent's that strong."

"I probably just didn't imitate it very well," Stevie said. "That would be par for the course, as far as Janey and I are concerned."

43

"Is she still being difficult?" Carole asked, putting down the hairbrush.

Stevie looked discouraged. "I'm supposed to be her big sister, and she doesn't want anything to do with me," she said. "She's really not very friendly. Yesterday after school I saw her at the stable, so I took her over to our good-luck horseshoe and told her all about the Pine Hollow tradition."

The others nodded. Every rider at Pine Hollow touched the good-luck horseshoe before beginning a ride. No rider at Pine Hollow had ever been seriously injured.

Stevie shook her head. "All she did was look at me and say, 'That's barmy,' and walk away! I don't even know what *barmy* means!"

"Nuts," Lisa translated. "It means she thinks it's a silly tradition."

"She's like that all the time," said Stevie. "Every time I tell her anything, she just gets this sullen look on her face and shrugs. The only thing she ever says is how Pine Hollow and Nickel aren't fancy enough for her. She wants everything to be fancy. I call that rude. Pine Hollow's not like one of those million-dollar show stables, but it's a great place, and if she wanted a million-dollar show stable, she should have gone to one."

Lisa scooted over by the bed. Stevie seemed really

upset. "She sure seemed bratty last Saturday," she said. "It can't be much fun to have to deal with her. I'm sorry."

Stevie sat next to her. "I'm sorry, too. I'm really trying. Every time I see her, I make myself go tell her something. I want to be a good big sister. Max will be disappointed if I'm not. But I can't be one if Janey won't let me. I don't think she wants to be a little sister. Or maybe she just doesn't like me. I don't know what to do."

"I guess since you're her big sister, you've got to keep trying," Carole said. "Maybe a few months at Pine Hollow will be good for her—cure her attitude. Anyway, Lisa and I will try to help you think of something."

"We'll do our best," Lisa promised. "The Saddle Club never fails. Unless she really is like Veronica, in which case, of course, curing her would be hopeless. But even then we'll try to help you endure her."

"Thanks," Stevie said. "I'd really appreciate it. Right now I haven't got a clue what to do."

"But I don't think we should have a Janey voice for *Horse Talk*," Carole said. "In the first place, I don't think making fun of her would help your relationship with her, Stevie—"

"Of course not!" Stevie said. "That was just for in here—"

45

"—and in the second place, you don't sound that much like her," Carole said. "But I bet you could do a good little boy. Try for one about Michael's age."

Stevie screwed up her face, thinking about her younger brother's voice.

Lisa lay back and looked at the ceiling. "I bet we sound just as strange to her as she does to us," she commented.

"Who?" said Stevie. "Janey? I doubt it."

"Sure," said Lisa. "If we went down to New Zealand, we'd be the strange ones."

"But we're not there, we're here," said Stevie.

"And we've got to finish these *Horse Talk* questions," Carole reminded them.

"Okay," Stevie asked in a Michael voice, "when can you first start training a horse?"

"Well," Carole said reflectively, "you can't start until it's *born* . . ."

LISA REACHED FOR a fresh sheet of paper. The floor of Stevie's bedroom was littered with lists of questions in Lisa's neat handwriting. Carole was making notes for the answers. She didn't write out exactly what she and Lisa would say, but she put down all the points they would need to make in their discussion.

"We've got twenty-five questions," Lisa said. "That should be enough, don't you think?"

Stevie and Carole thought about it. "Let's do a few

more," Carole said. "We're better off having too many than too few. I mean, what if we talk too fast? And we can save the extras for the week after."

Stevie thumbed through one of her dressage manuals. "Maybe a question about double bridles?" she suggested.

Carole shook her head. "You don't use a double bridle," she said. "None of us does. If it's too advanced for us, it's definitely too advanced for *Horse Talk*."

Stevie sighed and smiled. "I guess so. How about piaffe and passage?" Stevie had a passion for dressage, an elegant kind of riding that was similar to ballet. Double bridles were special bridles used in very high-level dressage, and piaffe and passage were two of the highest-level dressage moves.

"How about, 'What does the word *dressage* mean?'" Carole said. "That's a little closer to our audience's level."

"That's supposing we have an audience," Stevie countered. "So far, it's Mrs. Klemme, Max, and two people Lisa knows."

"Of those, only Max knows anything about dressage," Lisa said. "Carole's right." She wrote the question down while Stevie grumbled.

"Let me see the question list again," Stevie said. Lisa handed it to her.

The bedroom door flew open and Chad sauntered in.

"Get out of here!" Stevie said to him. She grabbed at his leg. Chad dodged her. "We're busy!"

Chad snatched one of the lists out of Stevie's hand. "What's this?"

"Give that back!" Stevie screeched. She grabbed his leg.

"Chad!" Lisa shouted. "Give it back!"

Carole jumped up and tried to get the list away from Chad. He held it away from her, kicked free of Stevie, and danced around to the other side of Stevie's desk. "Let's see," he said teasingly. "Maybe it's a love letter? No . . . it's just more horse stuff. Oh, wait! I get it. It's the *Horse Talk* talk!"

"Put it down, Chad," Carole pleaded. "It's ours."

"You miserable slime-bellied toad," Stevie added. She lunged toward Chad, but he held the list high in both hands.

"Come any closer and I'll tear it up," he threatened. They froze. " 'Hello, *Horse Talk*. Why do I need to take lessons to learn how to ride? Doesn't the horse do all the work?' " he read from the list. Chad's eyes lit up. "You're cheating!" he said.

"We are not," Lisa said indignantly. "We're just being prepared."

"Awfully prepared," Chad commented. "I'm sorry I missed the first show. I'll have to tune in for the second. Question sixteen: 'How much food do horses eat?' " He laughed. "What a stupid question! Here's another—"

"Give it *back*!" Stevie grabbed the list. Chad hung on to it, and the paper ripped in two. "Now you've done it!" Stevie shouted. Chad laughed again. He tossed his half of the list to Carole and ran out of the room.

"Horse Talk!" he said over his shoulder. "How many horses can dance on the head of a pin? Why don't horses play soccer? How many horses does it take to screw in a lightbulb?"

Lisa taped the pieces of the list back together. "Just ignore him," she suggested. "The more we react to him, the happier he is."

Stevie shook her head. "I don't like the look he just got in his eye," she said. "I've seen it before. He's not going to leave us alone."

Carole shut Stevie's bedroom door. "What could he possibly do?"

5

"HERE'S MY SAMANTHA voice," Stevie said to Lisa. "Tell me what you think. 'I'm afraid my horse was not treated well by his previous owner. Whenever I try to bridle him, he acts like I'm going to hit him. What should I do?'"

"Sounds fine," Lisa said briefly. She plugged in the last piece of radio equipment. It was Wednesday afternoon, ten minutes before *Horse Talk* was to begin, and she had butterflies in her stomach the size of pelicans. She could hardly think, much less listen to Stevie, who'd been doing voices for days. Where was that second set of headphones? For the third time, Lisa went through her mental checklist of radio and talk-show equipment. *Music tapes, equitation books, microphones . . .*

"I think it sounds a little too close to the Augusta voice," Stevie said. She looked through her list of questions worriedly. "Of course, Augusta and Janet are supposed to be close to the same age, but Janet's from the South, so shouldn't she speak—"

"Ask Carole," Lisa said. "She's in the locker room."

"Okay." Stevie wandered away, still muttering, and Lisa breathed a sigh of relief. Now, where was that dictionary?

Stevie nearly tripped in the doorway to the locker room. All her attention was focused on her paper. Trying to be twenty different people wasn't easy. In fact, it was impossible! She was sure she was going to sound the same no matter what. She didn't have Lisa's gift for acting. But she would certainly do her best.

" 'Whenever I try to bridle him,' " she repeated in a slightly different tone. "No, that's not right. 'Whenever I try to bridle him—' "

"Why don't you just ask Red to do it?" a snotty voice said. Stevie looked up from her paper to find Veronica looking down her long nose.

"What?" Stevie asked. She was so distracted she hadn't even heard what Veronica had said.

"I said, 'Why don't you just ask Red to do it?' " When Stevie still looked confused, Veronica added, "To bridle your horse. Never mind. It was a joke, but clearly some people are so wrapped up in themselves

51

that they can't see humor when it smacks them in the face."

Stevie stared at Veronica. Could the girl actually be trying to make a joke? And what was she talking about? Bridles? Red? "Huh?" Stevie asked, in her Patricia voice.

"You guys are getting *way* too involved in your little radio show," Veronica said, and huffed off.

"Carole," Stevie said, "listen to this. I think my Patricia voice is sliding into my Betty Sue voice. And the Janet voice is all messed up. What's wrong?"

Carole was searching through the pile of old clothes on the floor of her cubby. "I've lost my sixth sheet of answers," she said frantically. "I can't find it anywhere."

"I didn't think you were going to write out the answers," Stevie said. "I thought you and Lisa just had a short list of stuff to say back."

"Last night I couldn't sleep, so I got up and wrote the answers out for real," Carole explained. "I mean, what if I get nervous and totally blank?"

Stevie understood. "We weren't this nervous about the first show," she said. She helped Carole search through the pile.

"Here it is! Good." Carole wadded the sheet of paper into the pocket of her hooded sweatshirt. "We weren't this nervous because we were too clueless to realize what could go wrong," she told Stevie.

Stevie knew that that was true. "Let's go," she said. "By my watch, I ought to be heading for Max's home phone already. Look—I brought my boom box today. I'll be listening to the show from Max's living room, so I'll know what's happening even when I'm not on the phone."

They found Lisa hurrying Max out of the tack room. "I just need to find Barq's bridle—" Max was saying.

"Do it later!" Lisa said firmly. "Shoo!"

Carole felt her stomach flop and wondered how Lisa could be so calm.

"Two minutes," Lisa said. Carole nodded, and they took their places behind the table. Lisa took a deep breath and flipped the switch that would start the broadcast.

"Good afternoon, Willow Creek!" Carole said. "We're coming to you live from Pine Hollow. We're *Horse Talk*!" She recited the phone number. Exactly on cue, the phone rang.

"*Horse Talk*," said Lisa. "You're on the air."

"My name is Janet," said Stevie.

"Hello, Janet," Carole said. "How may we help you?"

"Well, I'm afraid my horse might have been mistreated by his previous owner . . ."

THE FIRST QUESTION went smoothly. Best of all, Lisa thought as she hung up the phone, it took nearly six minutes to answer. At that rate, leaving time for advertisements and station identification, they would only need eight questions an hour. Lisa read a short script about the school's radio project and played the first set of advertisements. Just as the tape finished, the phone rang again. It was Stevie, as Patricia, with prepared question number two. Carole answered it smoothly, and Lisa cut in with a short joke. All three of them laughed on cue.

Lisa hung up and repeated the phone number for the listening audience. The phone rang again, and Carole answered it. "*Horse Talk!* How may we help you?"

"My name is Augusta," said Stevie.

"Hello, Augusta!" said Carole and Lisa.

"I was wondering . . ."

THE SHOW PROGRESSED to the final fifteen minutes. Lisa eyed the clock with relief. *Horse Talk* was going fine, just as they had planned, but it had taken an awful lot of preparation, and she was tired. Carole looked strained. *Only two questions left to go,* Lisa wrote on a piece of paper. Carole nodded and smiled.

The phone rang again. "*Horse Talk!* How may we help you?"

"This is Roosevelt Franklin Godfreys the Third," announced an unfamiliar voice that was certainly not Stevie's.

Lisa waited for the caller to say more, but he didn't. "Uhh—Roosevelt Franklin what?"

"Godfreys the Third," replied the voice. "You can call me Rosie."

Carole recovered enough to say, "How can we help you, Rosie?" Lisa slapped her hand over her mouth to stop a giggle. *Rosie?*

"Well," drawled the caller, "you see, I have a horse. It's a very nice horse, but it's had several owners in the past. First when it was a baby it was owned by some very nice folks in Ohio. Then they sold it to a woman in Kentucky, and then I believe—but I'm not positive—that it came to Virginia, but not around here. I think it lived in Roanoke first, then Manassas, and finally it ended up with me. Or so I believe."

Lisa looked at Carole, who looked back. What was this about? "Go ahead," Lisa said into the microphone.

"Well," said Roosevelt Franklin Godfreys the Third, "the problem is, each owner messed up a different part of the horse. The first person made it inclined to kick with its back left foot only, but never from farther away than six feet. The second owner made it kick with the front right foot as well; the third owner made it tend to shimmy its hips; and the fourth cut my horse's tail off way too short. As a result of all this, my horse looks like a buzz-cut jitterbugging clog dancer, and I want to do dressage. What do you think I should do?"

"Uh," said Carole. She was pretty sure this was a joke, not a serious question, but what could she do? She was on the air. "Let its tail grow long," she said at last. "Don't cut it again." She looked at Lisa, who opened her eyes wider as if to say, "Don't ask me." "I think you'll find the ability to jitterbug an advantage in dressage," Carole added. "Any horse that can use its back end that well—"

"Thank you, caller!" Lisa said, and hung up the phone. Carole gave her a look of pure relief. Lisa looked at the clock, but all that silliness had hardly taken a minute of their time. The phone rang again.

"This is Julie," Stevie said, in a much more hurried voice than usual. "I want to learn to jump, but I'm worried about falling off. Do you have any advice?"

"Well, certainly," Lisa said, while Carole flipped through her papers to find the answer. "First of all, fear is something we all have to cope with . . ."

The question didn't last long enough. The very second that Lisa hung up the phone, it rang again. "This is Stonewall Pepperpot Maxwell the Second," another deep voice said. "I'm a friend of Roosevelt Franklin Godfreys the Third. You were so helpful with his question that I hoped you might answer mine."

"Sure," Lisa said. No matter what, it couldn't be more ridiculous than Rosie's question.

"My friends claim that when I'm riding my horse, it does all the work," the caller said. "But since I get hot

56

and sweaty and, I might add, extremely stinky whenever I ride, I'm pretty sure that I must be doing some work, too."

"Well, of course," Carole responded quickly. "Riding is excellent exercise—"

"What I'd like to know is this," the caller cut in. "Is there any way I can get the horse to do all the work? Because really, the stinkiness is gagging my whole family. It's so gross, you wouldn't believe. The way my riding boots smell—"

Lisa and Carole stared at each other. Lisa leaned closer to the microphone. "Buy some Odor-Eaters," she said.

"Next caller!" said Carole, hanging up the phone.

It rang again immediately. *"Horse Talk!"* Lisa said, hoping fervently that it was Stevie.

"Odor-Eaters might work for the boots, I admit. But what about those smelly riding breeches? And then there's all that manure. No matter what, I come home smelling like manure. . . ."

Lisa stared at the phone. They were trapped inside their own talk show with nine minutes of airtime left. Where was Stevie when they needed her?

THEY ANSWERED THREE more long-winded, hopelessly ridiculous questions before Carole cued the exit music and Lisa signed off. "Was that the same person over and over?" Lisa asked quietly.

57

"I couldn't tell," Carole said. "I think whoever it was thought they were pretty humorous."

"Well, I didn't!" Lisa felt ready to burst. "We're doing a lot of hard work here, and I don't like being made fun of! Manure!"

"I know," Carole said soberly. "At least we've only got to do this two more times. I wonder why Stevie quit calling? Look, here she comes."

Stevie stormed down the stable aisle. Her eyes glittered with rage. "I'll kill him!" she said. "I'm really going to do it this time. Didn't you guys recognize that cretin on the phone?"

Lisa and Carole shook their heads.

Stevie's face was crimson. "That was Chad!"

"HE ADMITS IT," Stevie said indignantly into the phone. She had called both Carole and Lisa (the Lakes had three-way calling) to tell them the news. "I accused him of calling our show and pretending to be five different people, and all he did was shrug and say he had a whole bunch of horsey questions that he needed to have answered. He was smiling, the creep! You could tell he thought he was just hilarious. And worse yet, he said he still had a few questions left!"

"Oh no!" Lisa groaned. "The ones he asked were hideous. Imagine what he might come up with for next week!"

"We've got to stop him," said Carole.

"I know," Stevie said with venom in her voice. "I've

59

been thinking of ways. I wish we could infect him with laryngitis. Or lock him in a jail cell, without a phone."

"Even criminals get to make one phone call," Lisa said with a weary laugh. She couldn't believe how ugly *Horse Talk* was becoming. At the start she'd thought it was a great idea. Now she just wished it was over.

"The worst part is that he really did get us," Carole said. "He didn't even do anything wrong. We're a talk show, and he called in with questions. We had to answer them. From his point of view, it was a perfect crime."

"They weren't even obvious crank questions," Lisa said in agreement. "I mean, if he'd called up and said, 'Is your refrigerator running?' we could have just hung up on him. But he's smart enough to ask actual questions about riding and horses."

"Strange, imaginary horses," Carole added. "Real horses don't shimmy their hips."

"I'm going to tell my parents, but I don't know if even that will do any good," Stevie said. "I'm sure they'll tell him to knock it off, but—"

"All he has to do is get a friend to call in for him," Carole interrupted.

"Sure," said Stevie. "That's what I would do."

"It's what we did do," Lisa reminded her. "We had you call in with questions because nobody else would. This whole talk show is just a disaster. We've got to do something, or Carole and I are going to be the laugh-ingstocks of the entire school."

"We'll come up with a plan," Carole said. "We've got all week." She was upset, but not as much as Lisa was. Carole didn't worry about school as much as Lisa did. What bothered her most was that here they were, willing and ready to teach people about horses, and no one wanted to learn. Carole knew that she would lis-ten to a radio show about horses. "Maybe we just need more publicity for *Horse Talk*, so that legitimate callers phone in."

"I was thinking more along the lines of posting Chad's naked baby pictures all over Fenton Hall," Stevie said. "Or maybe we could come up with some good reason for blackmail."

"Why don't we try talking to Chad?" Lisa suggested. "Maybe if we appeal to his better side—tell him how important this is to us—he'll knock it off."

"He doesn't have a better side," Stevie growled.

"Yeah," Carole said. "I mean, he might have a better side, but from what we've seen of Chad before, telling him how important *Horse Talk* is to us will just inspire him to bother us more. Maybe if we leave him alone, he'll leave us alone, too."

"I wouldn't count on that," Stevie said. "Revenge is the best option. But, like you said, we've got all week."

* * *

ON THURSDAY MORNING at school Lisa ran into Carole in the hallway. "How's it going so far?" she asked. Carole looked a little weary.

"You wouldn't believe the number of comments I've gotten about *Horse Talk*," Carole said. "I guess a lot more people listened to yesterday's show than the first one."

"I've gotten more comments, too," Lisa said. She rolled her eyes. "Some people told me they thought the show got more interesting right at the end. I couldn't tell if they were joking or just so ignorant about horses that they actually thought Chad's stupid pranks were serious questions."

"Angela Ashbury's in my algebra class," Carole said. "She rides with Cross County, and she figured out that it was all a setup. I mean, the first part. She knew we had the questions scripted, and she even realized that it was Stevie calling in."

"Only because she knows all three of us," Lisa said. "And she knows a lot about horses."

"But she thought we'd scripted the stupid questions, too," Carole reported. "She offered to help us come up with some ideas if we ran out for this week. She said, and I quote, 'We can't have the school's project sounding like an amateur production.' "

"But we *are* amateurs!" Lisa had to laugh. "Believe me, they couldn't pay me for this job."

"Girls!" Mrs. Klemme approached them. "I'm glad

to catch you both together," she said. "I just wanted to compliment you again on your show. You're really handling yourselves professionally—and you seemed to get some more interesting calls this week. Your program is really taking off. 'Good job!" She hurried down the hallway to her classroom. Lisa and Carole watched her go.

"Does she mean that?" Lisa asked. "I can't tell if she's being sincere or sarcastic."

"I think she means it," Carole decided. "Have you listened to any of the other shows? They mostly play music, and some of the DJs talk way too fast when they're on the air. You can't understand what they're saying. We have to talk the whole time, and we *are* handling the stupid calls. We're not hanging up or yelling at Chad on the air."

"I might have if I'd known it was him," Lisa said. "I guess we are doing some things right. But I'm dreading next week's show. I'm really afraid Mrs. Klemme is right."

"About what?" Carole shifted her backpack on her shoulder.

"About our show really taking off." Lisa sighed. "I have this feeling that Chad's going to be unstoppable."

TUESDAY AFTERNOON Stevie showed up at Pine Hollow in a foul mood. "We're in deep trouble," she told her friends.

"Oh no!" Lisa didn't even have to ask to know exactly what Stevie meant. All Thursday and Friday, word had spread around Fenton Hall, Stevie's school, about the excellent prank Chad had played on his sister. The Saddle Club had hoped the weekend would help settle things down. Instead, it only seemed to give the students more time to spread the word.

"Everyone thinks it's funny," Stevie reported now. She hung her school bag in her locker and started changing into her riding clothes. At least they had today's lesson to look forward to before tomorrow's disaster. "Everyone I ever played a joke on in my entire academic career finds this hilarious. Every student at Fenton Hall will be listening to you guys tomorrow, and I bet half of them will be calling in."

"But you aren't even a cohost," Lisa protested. "No one even knows you're involved." She pulled her boots on with more force than was necessary.

"They know," Stevie said. "I'm sorry, guys, but they know. Chad made sure of that."

Lisa rested her forehead against the bank of lockers. "What are we going to do?"

Carole finished pulling her hair back into a low ponytail. "Saddle Club meeting?" she suggested. Veronica waltzed in and started getting ready for the lesson, too. "In the tack room?" suggested Carole.

"Great." The Saddle Club hustled out the door. They didn't want Veronica to hear their plans.

"Stevie, maybe you can call in and never hang up the phone," Lisa suggested. "We could pretend that the phone was ringing—we could get an old bell or something—and you could just keep asking questions." She picked up Prancer's bridle and rubbed at some of the gunk on the edge of the bit. Why were bits so hard to keep clean? And why had she ever thought a radio show would be fun?

Carole sat down on one of the tack trunks. "If we did that, we'd have to script the whole thing," she protested.

"We've got questions left over from last time," Lisa reminded her.

"Yes, but—" Carole made a face. She tried to explain what was bothering her. "First of all, people are already catching on that we only had one caller. Now we know we're going to have lots of listeners. They'll all realize it's just Stevie, and if they call in and get a busy signal, they'll realize what we've done. Then we'll really look stupid.

"Plus," she continued, "if we take the phone off the hook, we'll be giving up on everyone. What if people really need our help with their horses and they can't get through? At least before, they had a chance."

"Carole," Lisa said, "I understand your concerns, but so far we have not received one single legitimate phone call. No one wants our help with their horses."

"Someone might," Carole said. "That was the point of doing this, wasn't it?"

"I guess so," Lisa said. "That, and it was supposed to be fun."

"Carole's right about everyone knowing we weren't taking real calls," Stevie said. "We could do it—it would sure be easier—but it would be like giving up. On ourselves."

Lisa shook her head. "Well, I *don't* want to do that. It's not our fault Chad is wrecking our show, but it would be our fault if we gave up. We have to try."

"The show goes on!" Stevie said, trying to muster up some enthusiasm. "I'm sorry it's my brother who's messing up your show."

"What can you do about it?" Lisa asked. "It's not your fault. At least this way, people are listening in."

Max poked his head into the tack room. "Stevie, there you are," he said. "Listen, Janey's joining your lesson today. Can you make sure she's got everything she needs?"

"Sure, Max." Stevie sighed. In her present mood she really didn't feel like talking to Janey. She still wasn't getting along with her.

"Good. Better hurry—we start in ten minutes."

"And Prancer's still a mess!" Lisa started grabbing tack. None of them had been paying attention to the time. Max hated it when his students were late.

"You check on Janey, we'll get Belle started for you," Carole instructed.

"Thanks." Stevie hurried down the aisle to the row of stalls where the ponies lived. She assumed Janey was still riding Nickel. What was Janey doing in their Tuesday lesson, anyway? Max tended to keep it to the advanced riders. The little kids rode on Wednesdays.

Stevie couldn't help feeling more and more irritated. She should have gotten Belle ready instead of worrying about the stupid radio show. Now she had to take care of Janey, who wouldn't be grateful for it, either. She was probably going to be late for her lesson.

"Hi, Stevie," Janey said when Stevie rushed into the stall. She had tied Nickel in the corner of the stall and groomed him, and she was just tightening the saddle girth.

"You missed some mud on his back leg," Stevie told her. "Look down here, see? You've always got to clean the mud off. He could have a sore or something underneath."

"I know," said Janey. "I just missed that spot. He rolled, so he was pretty dirty."

"And look, your girth isn't tight enough. You can't ride—"

"I *know*." This time Janey cut Stevie off. "I'm tightening it a little at a time. He doesn't mind it so much that way."

"Well, hurry up. It's almost time for the lesson, and Max yells like anything when we're late. Have you combed his mane? Can you get his bridle on okay, or do you need me to help you? Don't forget to clean his stall out after the lesson. And wipe out his water bucket, it looks dirty."

"Okay." Janey looked a little tight-lipped.

Stevie gave the pony another once-over. Nickel looked pretty good, and his tack was clean. Janey knew a lot about horses. Too bad she wasn't more friendly! "I've got to run," Stevie said. "See you in the ring— yell if you need me."

"Okay." Janey appeared to be speaking to the wall. Stevie sighed. Why was Janey so distant? Stevie didn't have time to think about it—she had to get her own horse ready.

"NO GYMNASTICS TODAY," Max said to them with a grin. They had finished warming their horses up on the flat and had now reached the part of the lesson Carole loved best: jumping. "We're going to take the lessons about body position that we learned over the gymnastic fences and use them to jump some bigger-than-average fences." As he spoke, Max walked around the arena. He'd already laid out a course of eight fences, but now he moved the top rails on each jump a little higher. Carole grinned. Max usually kept them to fairly low fences, but today everything in the arena looked more than three feet tall. This was going to be fun!

Max told them what order to jump the fences in. "Janey, you start," he instructed.

Until Max said that, Carole had forgotten that Janey was in their class. Janey picked up a canter and headed for the first fence, an impressive-looking Swedish oxer, and Carole had a sudden realization: Nickel was a pony! He was much shorter than any of the horses in the ring; to him, the jumps had to look huge! "What is Max thinking?" she whispered to Lisa.

Lisa shook her head. She was entranced by the expression of fierce concentration on Janey's face. If Janey had any doubts about Nickel's ability to jump such a large fence, she certainly didn't show it. She looked fearless.

Nickel snapped his knees under his chin and rounded his body over the fence with perfect form. He landed reaching into the bit, eager for the next jump but not rushing for it. Janey sat back a bit and balanced him perfectly. They jumped all eight fences with such authority that when they finished, Lisa and Carole broke out in cheers. Veronica sniffed, which meant she was highly impressed.

"Well *done!*" Max said. It was his highest compliment, and it was all he said, so he must have thought Janey's round was almost perfect. And, Lisa thought, it was. Janey and Nickel had moved in absolute harmony. Nickel was so calm he was usually trusted with beginning riders, but under Janey's command he looked ready to tackle any fence in the world. The Saddle Club did well during the lesson, but Janey was fabulous.

"Wow!" Carole said, turning to Stevie when the lesson was over and they were allowed to talk to each other. "Janey's amazing! How long has she been riding?"

Stevie had never guessed Janey could ride like that. She'd been as amazed during the lesson as her two friends. "I don't know," she said slowly. "All her life, I guess."

"But she can't be very old," Carole said.

"Yeah—I guess." Stevie was a little bit embarrassed. She'd never even asked Janey's age.

"I bet she has her own pony back in New Zealand," Lisa said. "She must have. I bet she events, with form like that. Stevie?"

Stevie shook her head. She could feel herself blushing. "I don't know," she said. "I guess. She doesn't talk about herself much."

Lisa nodded sympathetically. "She doesn't seem very friendly. It's too bad."

Stevie shook her head again. "I never asked how much riding she did before," she said. "I never asked if she had her own pony. I think—I think I've been doing most of the talking."

70

Suddenly Stevie felt bad about how she'd treated Janey. She'd acted as if Janey didn't know anything without finding out what she did know. She hadn't been a good big sister at all. Maybe Janey was a horrid little snob, a miniature Veronica. But maybe she wasn't. Veronica could never ride a horse as sympathetically as Janey had ridden Nickel.

Stevie resolved to make amends. She would go speak to—no, *with*—Janey as soon as she'd put Belle away. But that took a long time because Belle was sweating, and by the time Stevie was finished, Janey was already gone.

Stevie sighed. She'd make things right tomorrow. No—tomorrow was the call-in show. The horrible *Horse Talk*.

"READY?" LISA ASKED. She straightened the stack of horse books on the table.

"No," said Carole. "I'm not."

Lisa had been consciously keeping her shoulders square, but now she let them slump. "Me either." They had five minutes before *Horse Talk* was to begin. Lisa was starting to feel that an hour of dead air would be preferable to whatever was about to happen. Even the kids at her own school had started to talk about *Horse Talk*. Word had filtered over from Fenton Hall.

Max stopped on his way to the tack room, and Lisa didn't bother to try to throw him out. "Have courage," he said to them.

"What?" Carole asked. She'd been so busy thinking about jitterbugging fillies, she had hardly noticed him.

72

"Have courage," he said kindly. "You'll do fine, and it'll be over in an hour."

"Were you listening to the last show?" Lisa asked.

"Yep," he said, "and I'll be in the office listening to this one. Don't worry. You'll be fine."

"I am worried," Lisa said as soon as he had gone. "I think this will be miserable."

"Me too," said Carole.

"STEVIE," DEBORAH HISSED, coming down the stairs, "how many people did you invite into my living room? The baby is sleeping!" She waved her hands at the group of Pony Clubbers Stevie had rounded up from the stable. "Go on, go away! Back to the horses!"

"Deborah," Stevie said impatiently, "they're helping with the call-in show."

"We're going to call in," Corey explained, "so that Lisa and Carole won't feel all alone."

Deborah shook her head sympathetically. "I think that's nice of you, but I can't let you all stay. Maxi needs her nap. Stevie, you're it. Everybody else leaves."

"But Deborah!" Stevie protested in vain. The Pony Clubbers were already filing out the door. Everyone listened to Deborah just the way they listened to Max.

"And you can only make a few calls," Deborah continued. "I need to use the phone for some work myself. And whatever you do, keep your voice down."

"Okay," Stevie promised. She checked her watch.

Horse Talk was just about to begin. She switched her boom box on low and heard Lisa and Carole's theme music starting. She dialed the office number.

She got a busy signal. "Oh no!" Stevie whispered.

Over the radio, Stevie heard Carole say, "*Horse Talk!* Who's calling?"

"This is Andy," said a voice Stevie didn't recognize. It definitely wasn't Chad's. Stevie felt a surge of hope. Maybe it was a serious caller.

"Hi, Andy, I'm Carole."

"And I'm Lisa. Do you have a question for us?"

Stevie gritted her teeth. This first question would tell her if Chad and his friends were up to their tricks again.

"Um, yeah, I do. Could you train a horse to climb a tree?"

Stevie pressed her face into one of the pillows on the couch. If she didn't, she was afraid she would scream loudly enough to wake the baby.

"I don't think so," Carole replied calmly. "For one thing, an average horse weighs a thousand pounds. Thank you." Carole, Stevie realized, had hung up on Andy. Frantically Stevie redialed.

SHE GOT ANOTHER busy signal. The next caller was named Jamie. Jamie asked if horses could be trained to climb really big, strong trees.

The next caller asked if horses could be trained to climb the Eiffel Tower.

"Horses," Carole said through gritted teeth, "are not squirrels. They do not climb. They jump and run, and that's about it."

Lisa gave Carole's shoulder a sympathetic squeeze. She pressed the button to disconnect the caller. Immediately the phone rang again. Lisa hit the button. "We're not interested in any more climbing questions," she said.

"Um, right." This caller was a girl, and Lisa felt a bit better. Maybe this wasn't one of Chad's friends. "My name is Melanie, and my question takes a little bit of explaining," she said.

"Go ahead, Melanie," Lisa said encouragingly. She gave Carole a thumbs-up sign. A real caller at last! Carole shook her head warningly.

"Well, okay, so I was listening the other day to the caller who wanted to know if he could get his horse to do all the work, because riding made him so stinky—"

"I remember," Lisa said dryly.

Carole passed Lisa a note. *What's the name of Chad's new girlfriend?* it read.

"Okay, so I was thinking," the caller continued, "where does the stink come from? I mean, is it just from the exercise, or do horses stink, and does some of that rub off on the rider? If so, maybe you could get a big tall saddle that would hold you way off the horse's back, and then instead of blowing back on you, the stink would just sort of drift away. Under the saddle, do you get my drift?"

Lisa nodded to Carole. *Melanie*, she wrote on the note, and passed it back. "I have no idea what you're talking about," she said into the microphone. "Horses are the sweetest-smelling animals around, and I'd take the smell of three dozen horses any day over one jerky soccer-playing boy I know." She disconnected, but not before she heard Melanie start to laugh.

Lisa cradled her head in her hands. Why had she lost her temper? It would only make things worse.

The phone rang again. "What color is a horse in the dark?"

"The same color it is in the light," Carole snapped. She didn't want to lose her temper, either, but she was starting to feel it go. Didn't anyone in Willow Creek have a legitimate horse question? She patted Lisa's hand encouragingly while the phone rang again.

"If horses only eat grass and oats and stuff like that, why do we tell people that they eat like a horse? Nobody I know eats only oats."

No, Carole decided, no one in Willow Creek did.

The questions got worse and worse. Every time they finished one question, someone rang immediately with another.

"Let's talk about Willow Creek's middle-school radio project," Lisa said desperately. She ignored her short script and spoke at length, but when she had totally run out of words, she found that only two minutes had passed.

"Why doesn't Stevie call?" Carole whispered. Lisa rolled her eyes and tried to sound cheerful, or at least not furious, for the next caller. They both knew why Stevie wasn't calling. Every kid in Willow Creek was phoning in, and Stevie couldn't get through.

STEVIE COULD TELL from the strain in her friends' voices that if Carole and Lisa had to answer one more question about how horses did or did not compare to squirrels (no, horses did not hibernate; yes, they probably would eat nuts; no, they didn't bury nuts), they were going to break, go completely crazy, trash the barn, and probably get kicked out of the stable. She had to do something, but she couldn't. She called and called, and all she got was a busy signal.

"*Arrhgyh!*" Stevie finally yelled, slamming the phone down. From upstairs came the thin wail of a startled baby. "Sorry, Deborah," Stevie whispered.

"Out," Deborah said, pointing to the door. "Now."

STEVIE SLUNK INTO the barn and draped herself over a chair. "I've been evicted," she whispered under the cover of the commercial Carole had put on.

"Then we're doomed!" Lisa whispered back.

77

"We were already doomed," said Carole. *Horse Talk* was a failure, and they were doing a terrible job as its hosts. "*Horse Talk!* This is Carole!" she added when the phone rang as soon as the commercial ended.

"Hi, this is Roosevelt Franklin Godfreys the Third," said the caller.

"That's Chad," Stevie mouthed.

"Hi, Rosie," Lisa said. "You called in last week, didn't you?"

"Yeah, um, I did," said Chad. "I have another question."

"Let's hear it," Carole said. She rolled her eyes at Lisa.

"What's the difference between riding English and riding Western?"

"What?" Carole couldn't help sounding startled.

"You know, the way cowboys ride doesn't look like the way people ride when they jump and stuff."

"Right," Lisa said, grabbing the microphone and shooting Stevie a puzzled look *A real question! From Chad?* "Actually there aren't as many differences as there might seem to be . . ." The Saddle Club rode Western style when they visited their friend Kate out West, so they knew a lot about it. Lisa and Carole talked about riding styles for some time. It was a relief after comparing horses to squirrels.

"Okay, thanks," Chad said when they were finished.

"Um, I think you guys are doing a good job. It wouldn't be easy, doing a call-in show live and all."

"Thanks," Lisa whispered as she disconnected. Chad had started this whole mess. Was he feeling guilty?

The phone rang. "We're *Horse Talk*, and you're on the air!" Lisa said with renewed enthusiasm. Whatever Chad's motives, it was nice to have answered one real question.

"Hi," said the caller. "I took a pony ride at the zoo several years ago, and I have to say I didn't think it felt like work at all. I mean, I just sat there. I didn't notice any particular stink, either."

Carole rolled her eyes at Lisa. "Is that your question?" she asked.

"Oh, no," said the caller. "I've been listening to everybody talk about squirrels, and I was thinking, really, horses are a lot more like cows than they are like squirrels. So why don't people ride cows? Have you ever ridden a cow? And do you think cows could climb trees?"

SLOWLY THE HANDS of the clock dragged themselves toward five. The stupid questions rolled in as inexorably as a morning fog. Lisa felt utterly drained. "One more question," she mouthed to Carole, who nodded.

"Hi," said a voice that sounded like a very young girl. "Am I really on the radio?"

79

Lisa sighed. Another joke call. "Yes, you really are," she said. "Welcome to *Horse Talk*. What's your name?"

"Melissa," said the girl, "but everybody calls me Missa."

"Hi, Missa," Carole chimed in. "What can we help you with?"

"Well, see—" Missi began. Lisa sighed again. Another long-winded question. Those were her least favorite. At least the short ones you could get rid of quickly. "See, I live in just a regular house. I mean, in a neighborhood with just houses all around?"

"Yes?" Lisa prompted. She didn't understand what Missa meant.

"I mean, no barns or farms or anything. The library's on the corner—"

"We understand now," Carole cut in.

"Okay, so one morning this fall, it was on a Saturday, and I woke up really early 'cause I didn't have to go to school, and I looked out my window to the backyard, and there was a horse! So what should you do if you wake up and find a horse in your backyard?"

"Roll over and try to wake up again," Carole said. "Clearly you're still sleeping. I've had that dream a hundred times."

"But I'm serious!" said Missa. "It was standing right by my gym set."

"If it was fall, then it wasn't Christmas," said Lisa. "So was it your birthday?"

80

"Maybe you should start leaving carrots in your backyard," Carole suggested flippantly. "Like for the Easter Bunny. Maybe what you saw was the Thanksgiving Pony."

"But it was a *horse*," said Missa. "I saw it. I tried to catch it, but it ran away. I think it needed help."

"Whoa, look at the time!" Lisa said, disconnecting the phone. "Thanks for calling! We're *Horse Talk*, and believe it or not, we'll be back next week!" She cued their exit music and slumped her head to the desktop. "Oh, yuck," she said. "What a horrid afternoon."

Carole took off her headset and ran her fingers through her hair. "I think that was the longest hour of my entire life. Did you hear some of the things I said?"

"Did you hear some of the things the callers said?" Lisa asked with a groan. "We're never going to live this down."

"Guys," Stevie said. "That last call . . . What if it wasn't a joke? What if it was real?"

8

THE SADDLE CLUB packed the radio gear back into the boxes they kept it in and stacked them neatly in the corner of the tack room.

"I bet it wasn't real," Lisa said. "I hope it wasn't."

"Let's ask Max," suggested Carole. They walked to Max's office. Max was sitting in his desk chair surrounded by a group of younger riders, who were sitting on the floor. They were all cleaning tack, and all had obviously been listening to *Horse Talk*. Max's radio sat on the desk next to him. When The Saddle Club walked in, everyone in the office fell silent.

"Max," said Carole, "what if you woke up one morning and found a horse in your backyard?"

Max started to smile, but when he saw Carole's

thoughtful expression he answered her seriously. "I heard your last caller," he said. "I think you guys took the right approach answering her—I'm pretty sure that was supposed to be a joke." He gestured toward the radio. "No offense, but I don't think you should take any of those calls seriously. You guys handled yourselves well. You should be proud."

"We felt really sorry for you," said May. "I'm sorry Deborah kicked us out—we wanted to call up and tell everyone else to quit being jerks!"

"Rotten creeps," added Jasmine.

"We're just a little worried about that last call," Lisa repeated. "I know it sounded weird, but it wasn't totally stupid. What if it was real?"

"Nah," said May. "Horses don't just wander around the streets."

"Sometimes they do," Corey Takamura said. "Don't you guys remember when Sam ran away?" Samurai was Corey's pony, and he'd been missing once for several days. He'd come back on his own, and they'd never discovered just where he'd been. "Sam could've been roaming through people's backyards. He would have gone wherever there was good grass to eat," said Corey.

"That's right," said Janey. Stevie turned with a start. She hadn't spoken to her little sister since yesterday's lesson, and she hadn't noticed Janey in the office. "A horse wandered onto my family's sheep station once,"

Janey said. "We couldn't catch him, and he seemed pretty happy grazing with the sheep. He stayed a few weeks before we figured out who he belonged to."

"How did you figure it out?" Stevie asked.

Janey shrugged, but she also smiled. "We just asked around—you know, other farmers, vets, the feed store. Most people notice when one of their horses goes missing."

"Great idea," Stevie said with relief. "That's what we'll do. We'll call the other stables and the feed stores, and Judy." Judy was Pine Hollow's veterinarian.

"That would be fine," Max said. "A few phone calls can't hurt. But even if the call was real—even if this child thinks she saw a horse—I wouldn't get too worked up about it. In the first place, she might have seen a deer or a really big dog. And second, she said she saw it a while ago. Any escaped horse has probably found its way home long before this. I'm sure any horse would be fine now."

"Sure," Carole said. "We understand." She wandered out of the office and went to give Starlight a hug. Lisa and Stevie trailed after her.

"If Starlight ran away, I would just die," Carole said fiercely.

"I know," said Stevie. "But Starlight wouldn't run away. Horses know where their homes are. They've got great homing instincts, remember? So even if there was a missing horse, it probably did go home."

"That's right," Lisa said. Privately she was not convinced. The more she thought about the last call, the more she was convinced that the little girl's story was genuine. And if there was a loose horse . . . "The caller said she thought the horse needed help," Lisa said.

From the pained expressions on Stevie's and Carole's faces, Lisa knew they were worried about that, too.

"How would she know?" Carole said. "She was probably just saying that. She didn't seem to know much about horses."

"That's right," said Stevie. "I'm sure she didn't know what she was talking about. She probably saw a deer, anyway." Stevie tried to sound convincing. What were the odds that the call would lead to a genuine horse in distress? Stevie knew that they had to be small. Still, she worried. What if the horse needed them?

"I wish I hadn't hung up on Missa," Lisa said. "We could have talked to her after *Horse Talk* was over."

"It's not your fault," Carole said. "I thought she was a prank caller, too."

"We all did," said Stevie.

THEY WENT BACK to Max's office and asked if they could use the phone. First, they called Judy Barker. "I haven't heard of any missing horses," she said, "but I'll call the other vets in the area if you'd like." After that, they called the tack shop, the feed store, and a few of the other boarding stables in the area. All promised to ask around for news of a missing horse, but no one had heard of one so far.

"That's that," Stevie said as she hung up the phone. "No missing horse."

"I guess it must have been a prank," Lisa said. "At least we tried."

AT SCHOOL THE next morning, Mrs. Klemme stopped Carole and Lisa as they walked in the door together. "Nice job," she said.

Carole made a face. "You must be joking," said Lisa.

"I'm not," Mrs. Klemme answered. "That couldn't have been easy, and you two handled yourselves gracefully. Look at it this way: *Horse Talk* really has a lot of listeners!"

"I'll tell you how I'm looking at it," Carole said. "Only one week left!" Mrs. Klemme gave them an understanding smile.

ON FRIDAY NIGHT The Saddle Club had a sleepover at Lisa's house. Carole arrived first, and she and Lisa were setting the dinner table when Stevie burst in, wild with excitement. "We've got to call Judy!" she said.

"What happened?" Lisa cried.

"Is one of the horses sick?" Carole asked. "Starlight?"

86

"No!" Stevie threw down her overnight bag and grinned at them. "I just came from Pine Hollow. Judy left a message for us there. I tried to call her back already, but the line was busy. She found a missing horse! Our call was real!"

THE GIRLS TRIED three times to reach Judy, but her phone was busy each time. Since it wasn't an emergency, they didn't want to beep her. Finally, just before supper, they reached Judy's husband, who said that Judy was out on a call but would call them back at Lisa's house when she returned.

"He didn't know any details," Lisa said glumly, sliding into her place at the dinner table. The others nodded. After dinner they helped wash the dishes and clean up the kitchen. Still the phone didn't ring.

"Do you think we should try calling her again?" Stevie asked. They left the kitchen and went up to Lisa's room. "Maybe Judy's husband took Lisa's phone number down wrong."

Lisa shook her head. "He repeated it to me. He said Judy would be a while."

"Maybe we should watch a video," Carole suggested. "I'd say we should work on *Horse Talk*, but I don't know what we could do." Stevie nodded, and Lisa sighed. All the kids at both their schools had found the latest *Horse Talk* hilarious. Even the ones who clearly had no intention of calling in themselves, and who weren't especially interested in embarrassing The Saddle Club, seemed to have listened and found all the stupid questions amusing.

"The joke I keep hearing is, 'How is a cow like a squirrel? They're both on *Horse Talk!* '" said Lisa.

Carole rolled her eyes. "Every time I walk into my homeroom, three of the guys who sit in back yell, '*Horse Talk!* It's Carole!' I'm about to punch them in the nose."

"We sure don't need to write out any more questions," added Stevie. "I've still got all the ones from last week. I didn't get to use any of them."

"You'll be lucky if you use any this week, too," Lisa said. "I have a feeling we'll get just as many calls." She slumped into her armchair. "I never thought *Horse Talk* would be this popular. And I never thought I'd be sorry that it was."

Carole shook her head. "You shouldn't feel sorry—"

"Chad is such a jerk," interjected Stevie.

89

"—and if we find a missing horse—" continued Carole.

"We haven't found anything yet," Lisa said. The phone rang shrilly, and she grabbed it. "Hi, Judy! Hang on!" Lisa punched the speakerphone button. Her most recent gift from her mother had been one she really appreciated: a telephone with all the latest gadgets. "There. We're all here, Judy," she said, "and we can all hear you now."

"Hi," Judy said. "I called to tell you you guys were right. There *is* a horse missing around Pine Hollow. I don't know if it's the one your caller saw, but it could be."

"Fantastic!" said Stevie.

"It's quite a story," Judy continued. "One of the other vets around here takes care of the horses at Fox Meadow Farm."

"We've heard of it," Carole said. Fox Meadow was a boarding stable similar to Pine Hollow, on the other side of Willow Creek. It was supposed to be a nice stable.

"They have some students who compete in three-day eventing," Judy continued. Three-day eventing was a type of riding competition that included cross-country jumping. The Saddle Club sometimes enjoyed trying it at lower levels, but at higher levels it required a very athletic and specially trained horse. "One of them, a girl about your age, sold her first horse last summer and bought one that was more advanced. It was a gray quarter horse mare, and it had completed a preliminary three-day event."

"Wow," Lisa murmured. She knew that, though the word *preliminary* sounded easy, preliminary three-day events were tough.

"Yeah," Judy agreed. "It was a great little horse—named April Morning. The mare was up in Massachusetts, but the girl—her name is Samantha—and her parents looked at some videos of it and decided to buy it. The trainer at Fox Meadow knew the person in Massachusetts who owned the horse, and everyone thought it would be a great horse for Samantha.

"They arranged for April Morning to be shipped down to Fox Meadow. Unfortunately, the evening the horse was to arrive here, we had a really terrible thunderstorm. Do you remember, back in August?"

"The one where all the lights went out?" asked Stevie. She remembered, because she'd used the blackout as an excuse to try to roast hot dogs in her family's fireplace. The sticks hadn't been strong enough, and the hot dogs had fallen into the fire. They really blazed.

"I think so," said Judy. "Anyway, just outside Willow Creek, on the highway exit ramp, the truck and horse trailer skidded on the wet pavement and rolled into a ditch. When the rescue squad got there, the driver of the truck was unconscious. The trailer was pretty smashed up, and its door wouldn't open, but the rescuers couldn't hear any noises coming from inside it. They assumed that either it was empty or the horses inside it were dead."

"Oh no," said Carole.

"When the driver woke up, back at the hospital, he told them he had had one horse, April Morning, on board. So they called Samantha and her trainer and the vet who told me the story, and they all went out to the site of the crash. Because of the power outage, there were lots of emergencies, and nobody had gotten around to pulling the wreck out of the ditch.

"But the side of the trailer was open—it looked as if it had been kicked open—and April Morning was gone. There was a little bit of blood inside the trailer, but not much. Any other clues the mare might have left were washed out by the rain. They still haven't found her."

The Saddle Club looked at each other in stunned silence. It was an incredible story. Carole tried to imagine the desolation of buying a horse and then losing it before you ever got to know it.

"Girls?" said Judy. "Are you there?"

"We're here," said Lisa. "We're just trying to take it all in."

"Samantha and her family have been looking for April for over three months," said Judy. "Up until now, they've concentrated their search on the other side of Willow Creek."

"And we found her!" Carole said.

Judy hesitated. "You found a person who saw a horse," she corrected Carole gently. "It may or may not have been April Morning. After all this time, Samantha and her parents have pretty much given up hope. What color was the horse your listener saw?"

Lisa felt embarrassed. "We didn't ask," she said. "We assumed the call was another joke, until it was too late."

"I wouldn't get your hopes too high," Judy cautioned them. "The vet who saw the wreck said it was amazing that any horse had gotten out of it. April could have been injured badly enough that she died. Or someone could have found her and kept her without tracing her back to Samantha. August was a long time ago."

"I know," Carole said. "I guess it wouldn't be fair to get Samantha's hopes up."

"Why not?" asked Stevie. "She needs to know what we found out." Stevie's horse, Belle, had actually been stolen from a previous owner, and once they discovered this, it had been a long week before she'd known whether she'd be allowed to keep Belle. Stevie would've died if she hadn't known what was going on.

"I agree," Judy said. "Samantha knows what the odds are. In fact, I've already told her about you guys and *Horse Talk*. I said that you'd probably be at Pine Hollow tomorrow morning if she wanted to stop by."

Carole had to laugh. "Us be at Pine Hollow on a Saturday morning? I'd say that's a pretty good guess."

Judy laughed and said good-bye. Lisa reached up to turn the phone off, and the three members of The Saddle Club stared at each other for a moment. Then Lisa started to grin. "I guess I don't feel so bad about *Horse Talk* now," she said. "What if our show actually helps Samantha find her horse?"

Carole didn't look happy. "I'm just worried that it can't be the right horse," she said. "What are the odds of a horse surviving a crash like that and then living for months on its own?"

Lisa sat down on the floor and reached for a pad of paper. She always thought better when she was doodling. "First, I'd say they were separate odds," she said. "The odds of the horse surviving the crash may not have been very high, but we *know* the horse survived the crash. And we know that it kicked the side of the trailer out, so it couldn't have broken all four legs or anything like that."

"It still could have been badly hurt," Carole said.

"Well, sure," Stevie said. "But it might not have been. There isn't any way for us to know that."

"Then there are the odds of a horse living for three months on its own," Lisa continued.

94

"Now, that could happen," Carole admitted. "Remember the herds of wild horses out West?"

"Sure," Lisa said. "All horses need for survival is food and water, and they can find food anywhere there's enough grass."

"I've been thinking," Stevie said. "The caller—Missa—said she lives near the library, remember?" Carole and Lisa nodded. "That's not really too far from Pine Hollow. It's all subdivisions, but the back of the subdivisions border the woods that connect to the woods behind Pine Hollow." There were miles of trails in the hills behind Pine Hollow.

"So why wouldn't April come hang out with the Pine Hollow horses, the way the horse Janey found hung out with her family's sheep?" asked Carole. Horses were social animals, and they didn't like to be alone.

"Think about it," Stevie said. "There's a wire fence between Pine Hollow and the subdivisions. There are a couple of gates in the fence, but a horse couldn't unlatch them." Carole nodded. She remembered that Max was glad there were fences through part of the woods. It meant that any horse that might run away from Pine Hollow wouldn't be able to reach a highway or downtown Willow Creek.

"We'll talk to Samantha tomorrow," Carole said. "I hope April Morning isn't in danger." She was more and more convinced that Missa had seen April.

"If it is April, then she's survived a long time on her own," Lisa said comfortingly. "She'll be okay for another week."

After some discussion, they decided to watch a video after all. Lisa's mom had rented *Phar Lap*, an old film about an Australian racehorse. The Saddle Club had seen it three times already, even though the ending made them all cry. They went down to make popcorn, then hauled the VCR back up to Lisa's room. Lisa had her own TV.

"Stevie," Lisa said as she connected the cables to the back of the TV, "I've been thinking about Janey ever since Wednesday evening. Before she seemed like a real brat, but Wednesday she was different. She seemed like a really nice little kid. I mean, talking about her sheep station—she seemed friendly, and she didn't act shy at all. She really seems to know a lot about horses. I actually liked her."

Stevie flushed a little. "I know," she said. "She seemed like a different person to me on Wednesday, too. But I think I might know why we haven't been getting along." Stevie took a sip of her soda and tried to think how to explain. "I think I've been trying too hard to—well, not to tell Janey what to do, but something like that. I think I assumed she didn't know much, because she was younger and from a different country and all, and so I tried to tell her everything. I don't think I listened very much. She seemed like such

96

a brat right at first, but now I think that maybe she just felt uncomfortable in a new place."

Stevie sighed. "It's been bothering me," she admitted. "I was so busy being a *big* sister that I forgot to be a big *sister*. And then, when she didn't act very friendly at the start, I didn't act very friendly back. It kind of made me mad that she wasn't appreciating my help. I didn't bother to get to know her very well."

Stevie looked upset. Carole smiled. "I hope you're right, because I'd hate to think she was really like Veronica! I bet Janey *was* really overwhelmed at first. I bet Virginia is a lot different from New Zealand. Now that she's had a chance to get to know us, she's more herself."

Stevie understood what Carole was saying, but it didn't make her feel better. "Sure," she said. "Who wouldn't be overwhelmed, moving to a new country? Part of my job as a big sister was to make her feel at home, and part of making her feel at home probably involved listening to her and learning something about her. I just talked—too much horse talk!" Stevie laughed. "Maybe that was the problem all along—the radio show!"

"I wouldn't be surprised," Lisa said dryly. "Don't worry; in another week we'll be done."

"But I'll still be a big sister," Stevie said. "I'll be a better one now."

"We should have been more of a help," Carole said.

"I moved enough as a child. I should have remembered how that feels."

"We've been too busy with *Horse Talk,*" Lisa said. "We're sorry."

"That's okay," Stevie said. "Janey'll be here at least another month. We'll get another chance with her."

Lisa and Carole looked at each other and smiled. *At least Stevie has learned something valuable from all this mess,* Lisa thought. *It might not be because of* Horse Talk, *but it's about horse talk.* Lisa still wanted to think of her radio show as valuable. Instead, it seemed to be a bigger disaster every single week. Next Wednesday the transmitter would probably blow up just as some stupid eighth-grade boy called to ask how horses compared to emus. The explosion would probably set the tack room on fire. They would have to evacuate the horses from the stable, and Max would be so mad he would never let her ride Prancer again. Lisa sighed. "Maybe we'll find April Morning," she said.

Carole let out a matching sigh as the tape started to roll. She looked out Lisa's window at the dark, cold night. "I hope she's okay, wherever she is."

"WHY IS EVERYONE trying to mess up your radio show?" May Grover asked Lisa indignantly. They were sitting in Max's office along with the rest of the Pony Club. As soon as Max arrived, the meeting would begin.

"It's a joke," Lisa said wearily. "At least, it's someone's idea of a joke. It's kind of been snowballing lately."

"It's mean," May said, her eyes flashing. Lisa remembered that May had seemed lukewarm about the idea of a radio show at first, and she smiled. May seemed to understand what she was thinking. "You guys are going to a lot of trouble," she said. "People shouldn't try to mess you up. It's not *nice*."

Around the room, the other Pony Clubbers murmured agreement. Veronica sniffed. Lisa expected her to say something about the triviality of radio shows in general, and *Horse Talk* in particular, but Janey cut her off, saying loudly, "We'll all help, if we can." There was a chorus of cheers.

"Thanks," Stevie said quickly as Max came into the room. "Stay after the meeting, and we'll make plans."

Carole rolled her eyes happily at Lisa. They knew from the night before that Stevie didn't have any plans, but she had the entire meeting to come up with one, and Stevie usually thought fast under pressure.

"OKAY," SAID STEVIE when the official meeting was over, "what we'll do is something I call a Reverse Chad." She divided the Pony Clubbers into several groups. Each would work from a different house. "I'll give you all questions to ask," she said, "and your jobs will be to dial in as often as possible. Every time you hear a busy signal, hang up and dial again immediately. If enough of us do it, we'll be able to jam the phone lines and block most of the prank calls."

"Depends on how many people are trying to make prank calls," Carole muttered to Lisa. They were standing together at the back of the room.

"If we cut the pranks down by a quarter, I'd be grateful," Lisa replied. "At least we'd get a break from unremitting stupidity."

The office door opened, and a girl walked in. She was wearing blue jeans, tennis shoes, and a heavy jacket, but something about the way she seemed so comfortable in a stable—and, perhaps, the stirrup-leather marks running down the inside of her jeans—told Carole that the girl was a rider. "Can we help you?" Carole asked.

The girl turned toward them. Her face looked sad and hopeful at the same time. "Judy said I should ask for The Saddle Club," she said. "I'm Samantha Harding."

Stevie looked up. "I'll be right back," she said, excusing herself from the other Pony Clubbers. She joined Lisa and Carole in introducing themselves to Samantha.

"Call me Sam," the girl said. She flicked her short curly hair over her ears. "I heard you might know something about April."

"Let's talk in the locker room," Lisa suggested. She thought Sam might not like to tell her story with twenty-eight other kids listening in. They sat down on the locker room benches, and Stevie nudged the door shut with her toe.

"Did Judy tell you what we heard?" she asked. "It wasn't much." She related the story of Missa's telephone call.

"I'm sorry we didn't find out more information from her," Lisa said. She was a little ashamed of how little they knew. "We didn't get her last name, or where exactly she lives, so we can't track her down, and we

101

didn't find out what the horse looked like or if she saw it more than once."

"We thought the call was another prank until after the show ended and we had a chance to think about it," Carole said. Like Lisa, she felt a little embarrassed. She didn't want Sam to think that they didn't care about her horse. "The show was sort of awful. Everyone who called in was doing it for a joke—"

Sam held up her hand. "Don't feel bad," she said. "I listened to the first part of your show, and I had to turn it off. I don't know how you could stand to talk to all those idiots." She took a deep breath. "Most of them sounded like they wouldn't know a horse if it kicked them."

Sam reached into her jacket pocket. "I brought some pictures of April. I can't let you keep them, because they're all I have, but I thought you'd like to look at them." She held out two snapshots of a gray mare. One showed her standing still, without any tack; the other showed her leaping a large stone fence with impressive form.

"Wow," Lisa said. "She's gorgeous."

"Yes, I think so, too." Sam gave a bitter snort. "How would I know, though? I own this horse, and I've never even seen her except in a video and these photographs. I've never gotten to pet her or ride her. She was supposed to be my birthday present. I keep praying that we'll find her by Christmas."

102

Carole could feel Sam's pain. "We'll do whatever we can to help you find her," she promised.

"That's right," Lisa agreed quickly. "If Missa calls back this week, we'll get a lot more information out of her. We'll try to convince her to call back. This is our last week, you know. We'll have to make an announcement at the start of the show. I hope she'll be listening again." Lisa looked at Carole and Stevie to see what they thought. "Oh," she added, remembering Stevie's plans to jam the phone lines.

Stevie nodded, understanding. "We won't be able to call in," she said, "or Missa might not get through." She smiled at Sam. "I'll call off the Reverse Chad."

"The what?" Sam looked startled.

"Don't worry about it," Lisa said. "We've been having a little problem with Stevie's brother. That's why we've had so many prank calls."

"We've been having a big problem," Carole corrected her. "And it's still a problem. If Chad and his friends call in the way they did last time, Missa might not get through, either. Instead of a Reverse Chad, we'll have our usual Normal Chad—that's bad."

"I could kill him," Stevie fumed. "I can't believe my brother managed to make this much of a mess. Maybe we could put him in jail. I'm definitely paying him back for this."

"And all his friends, too?" Lisa asked. "We could get your parents to lock Chad in his room, maybe, but we can't keep every middle-school student in Willow Creek away from the phone. And don't forget, it was Chad who called in with a real question. I don't think he planned to have his prank get carried so far." She wished once again that they had spoken to Chad when he had first started calling. Now it was definitely too late; too many people were involved.

"He should have," Stevie said. "He should have thought things through."

Lisa had to laugh, thinking about how seldom Stevie thought her own pranks through. Then she sighed. "Maybe the joke will have worn off by Wednesday. Maybe they'll have forgotten about us."

"I hope so," Sam said softly. "If April is still alive, it's really important that we find her soon."

"We'll do what we can," Carole assured her. She shot a look at Stevie. "We're not worrying about revenge this Wednesday. The only thing that matters is finding your horse."

"Of course," Stevie agreed. "And on Thursday we'll murder Chad."

They went back into the office and Stevie called off the Reverse Chad.

"Maybe it'll help if we tell them about April," Lisa whispered to Sam. "Do you mind?"

"Of course not," said Sam. "Anything that might help."

104

Stevie told the Pony Clubbers the story of the missing horse, and Sam passed her photographs around.

Lisa urged everyone to spread the news. "If the kids at school know why this is important, maybe they won't mess up the show," she said.

Polly Giacomin looked doubtful. She was in Lisa's grade. "The ones that are doing this to you aren't exactly considerate, or interested in horses," she said. "I think even when we tell them it's serious, they'll just laugh."

"But we will tell them," added Adam, one of the few boys in the Pony Club. "It certainly can't hurt."

"Thanks," Sam said. "It's really important that we find her."

As the other kids left the room, Janey came up to Sam and shyly slid her hand into the older girl's. "I know you must feel just awful," she said. "My Fancy's not even lost, I know she's safe at home with our caretakers, but I can't stop worrying about her."

Stevie stared at her little sister. A wave of realization swept over her. "You've got your own pony," she said, "named Fancy." She couldn't believe how stupid she felt. All the time Janey had been muttering about ponies being fancy, Stevie had thought she was saying that the Pine Hollow ponies weren't well bred.

"Of course," Janey said, looking amazed. "I've told you all about her."

"Right," Stevie said, flushing a little. "I just didn't realize that her name was Fancy." No wonder Janey hadn't taken to Nickel right away! She was homesick for her own pony!

"Fancy Free," Janey explained. "She's a Welsh cob, like Corey's pony, only she's a chestnut. I've had her three years. Every night at home I go out to the barn and feed her a carrot, right before I go to sleep. I can't sleep well here, because I keep worrying that Mr. Durgies has forgotten her carrot. What if Fancy thinks I don't love her anymore? What if she misses me something dreadful? I told her I'd be back before autumn, but I don't know if she understood. But she's a very smart pony."

Janey sounded anguished. Without thinking, Stevie leaned over and gave the little girl a hug. Janey hugged Stevie back tightly. "It won't be so long," Stevie said soothingly. "Max said you were only going to be here a few months. It won't be autumn before you see her again."

Janey laughed a somewhat shaky laugh. "Yes, it will," she said. "Right now in New Zealand it's the start of summer. By the time I go home, it'll be spring here and autumn there. I'm going to miss summer entirely."

Stevie was horrified. "That's terrible! You'll have to go right back to school!"

"Don't I know it," Janey said.

"But your pony will be there waiting for you," Carole said. "She won't have forgotten you."

"Do you really think so? Four months is a long time."

Sam leaned on the desk. "I'm sure of it," Sam said. "Fancy knows you better than she knows anyone else. Your smell, your voice—she knows everything about you. She'll remember that you bring her carrots. She won't forget."

Sam paused. "Four months is about how long April has been missing," she added. "I wonder what she remembers. She can't have forgotten me, since she never knew me."

"Do you want to go see Nickel, the pony I'm riding here?" Janey asked her. "He's quite a good jumper."

Carole had to laugh. She had never thought of Nickel as a good jumper until she had seen Janey riding him.

"Sure," said Sam.

"We'll all go," offered Lisa. "And maybe, Sam, you'd like to take a trail ride. I'm sure Max wouldn't mind."

"With the four of us," Stevie added. Janey beamed.

Sam shook her head. "My mom's coming to pick me up in fifteen minutes. I've actually got a riding lesson at Fox Meadow. I've been riding school horses, since I don't have April."

They came to Nickel's stall, and the pony whickered lovingly at Janey. "Here's your carrot, good boy," Janey said, pulling one from her pocket.

"You'll spoil him rotten," Stevie said.

Janey's eyes opened wide. "Ponies are like babies," she said. "You can't spoil them by loving them."

"It's a good thing," cracked Lisa, "or Belle and Starlight would be the most spoiled horses on earth!" They all laughed, even Sam. They introduced her to the other horses in the stable, including Belle, Starlight, and Prancer.

"Would you mind if I came on Wednesday and sat in on your show?" Sam asked. She held her hand out for Belle to sniff, then patted the mare's soft neck. "I'd like to be able to ask some questions myself, if someone calls in who might have seen April."

"Of course," Carole said instantly. "If you think that might help, we'd be happy to have you with us."

"We've got to find her before the weather gets too cold," Sam said.

Lisa frowned. "You've said that several times," she said. "But if April survived the crash—if she is wandering around loose—why is it so important to find her now? If she's doing okay on her own, wouldn't she keep doing okay?" Lisa knew that winter weather didn't bother horses any more than it bothered wild animals. Horses grew thick winter coats, and as long as they could find food and water, they would be fine.

Sam looked surprised by Lisa's question. Her eyes opened wide. "I guess I haven't told you," she said. "I didn't realize that I didn't say it right away. April might do fine if she were on her own, but she's not. Her owner had her bred late last winter. She's pregnant."

"I DON'T KNOW what to do," Lisa said. "I'm panicking. Really, I am." It was the night before the last *Horse Talk*, and she had gotten into a fluster just thinking about the show. She had called the rest of The Saddle Club.

"Shhh," Carole said soothingly. "It'll be okay. Or even if it won't, there's nothing you can do about it."

Lisa gave a short laugh. "Thanks. That certainly makes me feel better."

"What exactly are you panicking about?" Stevie asked.

"The whole thing," said Lisa. "What if *Horse Talk* is even worse than last week? What if I open my mouth and can't think of a single word to say? What if—this is the worst—what if Missa doesn't call back?"

110

"Great," said Carole. "Now you're making me worried."

"Sorry!"

"Listen," Stevie said softly. "There's no use worrying. We're as prepared as we can be, and we can't control what Chad or Missa or anyone else does."

"I know," Lisa said. "I just wish this didn't matter so much."

"When I think of April's poor little foal . . . ," agreed Carole. April's pregnancy made Sam's urgency perfectly understandable. Most horses didn't give birth until spring; a foal born in the winter needed special protection from the cold. Out in the wild, it would probably not survive.

"Don't," groaned Lisa. "That only makes me feel worse."

"We can't do anything about it now," Stevie said. "We'll do our best tomorrow."

"I suppose," Lisa said. Talking to her friends always made her feel better, even when they couldn't change what was bothering her.

"We will do our best," Carole promised.

THE NEXT AFTERNOON, the panic butterflies in Lisa's stomach had been replaced by a new and more insidious sort of insect, one that seemed to be tying her stomach into a series of tight knots. Sam sat bolt upright in her chair while The Saddle Club set up the

111

equipment for *Horse Talk*. Lisa, looking at Sam's hopeful expression, knew full well how crucial this show could be. She could hardly stand the pressure.

"I brought a map," Sam said. "So we could figure out where Missa lives."

"Good," said Carole. Like Lisa, she could hardly stand to look at Sam. *Horse Talk* had started out as something fun to do. Then the prank had turned it into something awful, and now it seemed much too important for a school project. The life of a foal could depend on it!

"Did you work out what you were going to say?" she asked Lisa in an undertone. They had agreed that Lisa would begin the program.

"No," Lisa said. "I mean, yes. I thought about it, but whenever I tried to write anything down, it didn't come out right. So I'm going to just talk."

"Sounds fine," Carole said, giving her an encouraging squeeze of the hand. She and Lisa took their places behind the table. The clock said three minutes to four.

Stevie plugged in the last electrical cord. "Are you sure you don't want me to go over to Mrs. Reg's?" she asked. "I could try to get a few calls in. Maybe I could ask questions that would encourage other people to call."

Lisa shook her head. "I don't think so. We've got to give Missa every chance."

Sam looked at the clock. "Almost time."

Carole cued *Horse Talk*'s opening music. Lisa moved the microphone closer to her mouth and let the last note fade. "We're *Horse Talk*," she said, in a quieter, more compelling voice than she had used so far. "We're coming to you live from Pine Hollow Stables with a special mission today. At the end of our last show, a young girl named Missa called in to report a runaway horse she'd seen. We have reason to believe that the horse might be April Morning, a pregnant quarter horse that has been missing in the area since August."

Lisa sounded as professional as a television anchor. Carole was impressed. "We need to find this horse," Carole said urgently. "Anyone around Pine Hollow who has seen or thinks they might have seen a loose horse needs to call us right now. And Missa, please call back. We want to talk to you." Carole repeated the phone number twice.

Lisa took a deep breath. She was about to add something else to what Carole had said when the phone rang. Lisa answered. *"Horse Talk,"* she said. "Thanks for calling."

"Hi," said a voice that sounded like a boy's. "I'd like to speak to Carole. My name is Pinkerton Pinkley, and I've got a horse that can climb—"

"Now, *look*." Lisa interrupted "Pinkerton Pinkley" in midsentence. "You and people like you are *wasting our time*. That was fine last week, when we didn't have

113

anything else to do. This week we've got a missing horse to find, we have only one hour to try to find it in, and you're taking up our phone line with nonsense. We don't have time for it."

Lisa hung up the phone, but not before they could hear a muffled "Sorry" coming out of it. Lisa repeated the bulk of her earlier message. "Missa, please call back," she added.

The phone rang again. This time it wasn't Missa or a prank, it was an adult who said he'd seen a mysterious horse several times. "It's always at night, when I'm coming home from work," he added. "I work the late shift. The horse is eating grass by the side of the road. It's a big white horse. The first time I saw it, I thought it was a ghost."

"Gray," Lisa murmured. Most people mistakenly called gray horses white.

"Yeah," the guy said. "It was spooky-looking. But it was definitely a real horse. I tried to catch it once, but it ran away."

"Great," Carole said. "It sounds like it could be the right horse. What road did you see it on?" The caller named an intersection not too far from Pine Hollow.

Sam circled it on the map. "That's not far from the library, either," she whispered excitedly. "Fantastic!"

"Thank you for calling, sir. Please, call in, anyone else who has seen this horse," Lisa implored. The phone rang again. In quick succession, two other callers reported that they had seen a horse—white or gray—somewhere around the edge of the woods near the library. Both had seen the horse within the past two weeks, and both said that the horse ran away when approached.

"Ask if it was limping," Sam whispered while Carole was talking to the second caller. "Ask if it looked hurt."

"No," the caller said. "Looked fine to me."

Sam beamed. She and Stevie spread the map out on the one clear spot on the table and started marking the places where the horse had been seen. They were all in the same general area.

"Sounds like we're on the trail of a horse!" Lisa said into the microphone. "Please, anyone, if you've seen this mystery animal, call us now." She repeated the phone number, but before she was halfway through, the phone rang again. Carole jabbed the button to answer it.

"This is Missa." The little girl sounded excited. "I called last week, remember?"

"Missa!" Carole was thrilled. Sam and Stevie gave each other high fives. "Of course we remember. Tell us about the horse you saw."

"Well, remember you told me to put carrots in the backyard?"

Carole didn't remember, but she went along with it. "Sure. So what color—"

115

"Well, guess what?" Missa's voice squeaked with delight. "I did it, just like you said, and it worked!"

"What worked?" Carole asked.

Lisa thought she understood. "The horse came back?" she asked.

"Yes," said Missa, "and he's right here now! He's eating them!"

"What's she look like?" Sam demanded. "Can you see her?"

"Sure. Is it a girl horse? She's white on her back and has black legs, and funny shadow-marks on her behind."

"Dapples," Sam explained. "She's a dappled gray."

"She must really love carrots," Missa said. "Since you told me to last week, I've been putting carrots out every day, and she's been coming to eat them. Yesterday she let me touch her nose."

Sam looked ready to burst. Lisa couldn't believe their luck. Even though they hadn't listened to Missa last week, she had listened to them!

"Okay," Sam said breathlessly, "look right now at her hip. Can you see her left side? Does she have any kind of a marking there?"

"She's got a funny spot that looks like a smiley face," Missa reported. "It's dark."

Sam shoved one of the photographs of April across the table to Carole. She pointed to the mark on April's hip. "That's a brand," Carole explained.

116

"That's the right horse, all right. Now, Missa, you need to tell us your address."

"Come on!" Stevie grabbed Sam's arm and pulled her into the tack room. "We'll go get her—it's not far cross-country." She grabbed Belle's bridle.

Max came in, followed by Janey. "I thought I'd find you here," he said when he saw Sam and Stevie. "Take Calypso, she's fast."

"Thanks!" Stevie grabbed the other bridle from its peg. "We won't bother with saddles—Sam?"

"Bareback's fine with me," Sam said.

Janey looked at Stevie. "Can I come?"

"Sure," Stevie said. "Hurry!"

Janey was trotting Nickel down the stable aisle from one direction just as Stevie and Sam were coming from the other. Stevie and Janey quickly touched the Pine Hollow horseshoe for good luck and told Sam to touch it, too. "I grabbed Belle's halter for April," Stevie said. Sam took it and slung it over her arm. "What's the address?"

Lisa hurried down the aisle, looking stricken. "Here," Lisa said, handing Stevie a slip of paper. "But April's gone! While Missa was talking to us, April left!"

"Oh no!" Sam said from the aisle.

"We'll find her!" Stevie promised. "We know where she was a minute ago." She had a sudden idea. Thrusting Belle's reins into Janey's hands, she ran down to

117

Max's office and opened the big cabinet where he kept his show supplies. Along with the PA system they used whenever they had an event at Pine Hollow, Max kept a pair of walkie-talkies. Stevie grabbed them. "Here," she said to Carole. "See if you two can track the horse down, and let us know where to go." Stevie took the other walkie-talkie with her.

Stevie and Sam had to use the mounting block to scramble onto their horses' bare backs, but Janey managed to vault aboard the smaller Nickel. In a moment they were away from the buildings and galloping across the field. "If we ride fast, it'll take us about ten minutes to get to where April was," Stevie shouted. Sam nodded. They knew they had to hurry. All the time they were riding toward April, April could be moving away from them.

"Are you there, Stevie?" Carole asked over a hiss of static. Stevie managed to press the button on the walkie-talkie and hold it against her ear.

"We're here," she said. "We're heading out."

"Just checking," Carole said. "They can hear you on the air."

"We're *Horse Talk*, coming to you live from Pine Hollow with an exciting search and rescue in progress," Lisa said. "We've been looking for a missing mare, April Morning, and she was just seen in one of our listeners' backyards." Lisa gave Missa's address. "A

118

mounted rescue crew is on the way, but the mare is moving. Any listeners who live in the area, please look out your windows now. If you see a horse, call in. We need to find this mare."

"I see her!" said a caller who sounded like an elderly woman. "She's walking right across the middle of my backyard!"

"Which direction?" Carole asked, at the same time as Lisa asked, "What's your address?" The lady told them both. "Sounds like April's heading back toward the woods," Lisa commented.

"Stevie, where are you?" Carole asked. She reported the latest movements.

Stevie, listening, looked across the field. Galloping bareback was one of the greatest thrills on earth. Bareback riding required very good balance, since there was no saddle to help the rider stay on. However, it also allowed the rider to really feel the motion of the horse she was riding—it was almost like being part of the horse. Beside Stevie, Nickel and Janey were flying, and Sam on Calypso was close on their heels.

"We're catty-corner from the gate that goes into the woods," Stevie said. "We'll be in the subdivision in three minutes." She took the walkie-talkie away from her ear.

"Less," Janey commented, "if we don't take the time to open that gate."

119

"You mean jump it?" Stevie asked. The wooden gate was solid, certainly jumpable, but it looked at least four feet high. It looked huge.

"It'll save time," Sam said. Stevie remembered that Sam was an event rider, and Calypso, a Thoroughbred, was a skilled jumper. They could probably take the fence, and she felt as if she could, too. But she was responsible for her little sister.

"On Nickel?" she asked Janey as they galloped across the field.

Janey grinned. "It looks smaller than the gate on our sheep pasture at home, and I jump that all the time," she said. When Stevie hesitated, she added, "Don't tell Max, but May and I were playing puissance the other day, and Nickel jumped a rail five feet high."

Stevie had to laugh. "You know best," she said. She pointed Belle toward the gate. "Hang on tight!"

Inside the stable, the phone was ringing off the hook. Several more people had seen April, who seemed to be taking a tour of the subdivision back-yards. Lisa took the calls and wrote down the addresses. Some of the addresses weren't making sense. Lisa was afraid that some of the calls must be false alarms. But how could she tell? Carole kept in touch with Stevie and traced their progress on the map. "I think they jumped that corner gate," she reported to Lisa.

Lisa grinned. "Bet it saved time." She was beginning

to worry a little bit about not having enough time. For once, *Horse Talk* was flying by.

"We're in the subdivision now," Stevie reported via the walkie-talkie. "We've slowed to a walk. A lot of people are out on their front lawns watching us."

"We're famous," Janey said cheerily, waving left and right.

"Turn left on Rosewood Street," Carole said. "The horse should be—"

"No, wait!" Lisa, taking another call, waved to Carole. "The horse went through some backyards!"

"Can you cut through to Oakdale?" Carole asked Stevie.

"Where's Oakdale?" Stevie asked.

"Can't do it," Sam said. "There's a swimming pool in the way."

"Okay, turn left at the swimming pool, then right. You should be able to see her once you get around the corner," Carole said.

Sam looked anxiously from side to side. "I don't see her."

"She took off!" Lisa said. "She's gone back the other way! Listeners, please don't run after the horse! You'll just make her run away!"

Stevie, Sam, and Janey looked at the crowded subdivision streets. "We can't lose her now," Sam said, tears in her eyes.

"We won't," Stevie promised.

"*Horse Talk!*" Lisa answered the phone.

"Hey," said a man's voice. "You know the missing horse you guys are tailing? My wife just caught it in our backyard. She's leading it round to the front."

Lisa gestured frantically to Carole. "Tell Stevie!"

Carole pushed the button in on the walkie-talkie, but Stevie preempted her. "We see her!" Stevie shouted. Ahead of them, standing surrounded by people on someone's front lawn, an elegant gray mare lifted her head as she sensed the approaching horses. The mare's nostrils widened, and she gave a loud, excited whinny.

Sam galloped Calypso over the last twenty feet. Stevie followed. She kept her finger on the Transmit button and held the walkie-talkie high. Listeners across Willow Creek heard Sam's joyful shout: "April! *You're alive!*"

STEVIE PUT THE walkie-talkie back to her mouth. "This is Stevie Lake, reporting live for *Horse Talk*. The missing horse has been found." She clicked the walkie-talkie off.

At Pine Hollow, the click was followed by a moment of silence. Neither Carole nor Lisa knew exactly what to say next. Carole had tears in her eyes. Lisa couldn't believe what had just happened. She leaned over and spoke into the microphone. "Thank you, Willow Creek. On behalf of Samantha Harding, owner of April Morning, the horse that survived a terrible crash and has been missing for almost four months but that was found here this afternoon, thanks very much to all of you who listened and called in. My cohost, Carole Hanson, joins me in thanking also the many people who supported the radio school project and our show, *Horse Talk*, especially our instructor, Max Regnery, who owns Pine Hollow. This is our final show."

"Thanks also to the many sponsors who are making the radio school project possible," Carole added smoothly. "We didn't want to interrupt our live, breaking coverage of the rescue of April Morning, so we'll play all our advertisements now." She slid the ad tape into the deck and clicked off the microphone.

Lisa laughed. "I forgot all about the advertisements! How long will they last if we run them all together?"

Carole looked at the clock. "Too long. They'll probably all get on, but we won't be able to play our exit music." She grinned at Lisa. "I'd say, though, that we made our exit in style."

"Saddle Club style," said Lisa. She looked at the radio equipment. "I can't believe we ended like that."

"It's a lot better than the way we began," said Carole. "I think I'll call Judy and ask her if she can come here. April ought to be examined right away."

Lisa nodded. "I'll go find Max and see if he can take April back to Fox Meadow in his trailer."

She stepped out of the stable just in time to see Judy pull up into the drive. "Carole!" Lisa called. "She's already here!"

Carole joined Lisa, and they ran to greet Judy. "We

were just going to call you!" Carole said. "We've got a horse coming—"

"I know." Judy was grinning from ear to ear. "I was listening on my radio in the truck. Quite a story! How long will it take for them to get back here?"

"Not too long," Lisa said. She muttered to Carole, "I hope they don't try to jump that gate leading April."

"Not in her condition," Carole agreed.

"I'll find Max," Lisa said, remembering her initial intention.

Judy pointed. "He's right there."

Lisa turned and saw Max hooking his horse trailer to his pickup truck. "Max! Did you hear?"

Like Judy, he was smiling. "Of course I heard! We were listening in the office. You guys did great!"

"Oh." Lisa blushed. "It wasn't us, it was everyone who called in. They found the horse—we just followed their lead."

"Your show attracted a lot of listeners," Max said with a wicked grin.

"Don't remind me," Lisa said.

"Look!" said Carole. "Here they come!"

Nickel streaked into the yard with Janey whooping like an Amazon princess on his back. They slid to a stop right in front of Max, and Lisa wondered briefly if the pony would ever be the same again. How could he revert to giving lessons to beginners after a season with Janey? Lisa decided it was Max's problem.

125

Stevie followed on Belle. She'd gathered her into as close a semblance to a collected dressage trot as she could manage bareback, and she made Belle prance and turn circles around Sam.

But everyone was watching Sam. Riding Calypso, she sat tall and proud while tears of happiness glistened on her cheeks. Sam was leading April Morning. The gray mare seemed happy to be in the company of other horses again. She trotted briskly, her ears pricked forward and her tail held high.

Carole couldn't help counting the cadence of April's trot: one-two, one-two, her steps as even and firm as they should be. So the accident hadn't left April permanently lame.

Sam slid off Calypso and hugged April. Lisa came up to take Calypso, and Sam hugged her, too. Then Sam hugged Stevie, Carole, and Janey; then she hugged Judy and Max; last, she hugged April again. "She looks so great," she said. "Can you believe it?"

"She's prettier than her photograph," Carole said honestly. "She's a fantastic-looking horse."

"I can't wait to see her baby," Stevie added.

Sam patted April's midsection. "She still looks pregnant; that's one good sign." None of The Saddle Club had mentioned it, but they all knew that the mare could have miscarried because of the crash.

Judy came forward with her stethoscope. "Let me listen." April held still while Judy pressed the stetho-

126

scope along her belly. Judy's grin told The Saddle Club what they wanted to know before Judy said a word. "The foal's got a nice, healthy heartbeat," she said. Sam threw her arms around April again, and The Saddle Club gave each other a high fifteen.

"She's got a scar back here," Judy reported, continuing her examination. "She could have used stitches on it, probably, but other than that, she seems fine. She'll need some blood work and a more thorough exam in a few days, but she's in amazing condition, all things considered."

Another car pulled up in the driveway. "Mom!" Sam called out. "Dad! We found her!"

Sam's parents got out and joined the celebration. "We heard on the radio," Mrs. Harding said. "I'm so thrilled!" She hugged her daughter.

"Where are the young ladies who put on that radio show?" asked Mr. Harding. Sam introduced him to The Saddle Club. He pulled out his wallet. "I think you ladies deserve a reward."

"Oh, no." Carole shook her head. "Not for finding April. We'd always help a horse. We don't need a reward."

"We're grateful to April for helping us with our radio show," Lisa added. "It was much more interesting today."

Mr. Harding laughed. "It was certainly interesting." He put most of his money away, but he insisted that they take enough to buy themselves an ice cream. "Don't think of it as a reward," he said. "Think of it as a gift from Sam and April."

"And you'll have to come see the foal when it's born," Sam added.

"We'd love to," said Carole. "You'll have to come back and visit, too. Come ride with us sometime."

"I'd like that." Sam turned to her horse. "Come on, darling, let's get you home."

"Here," Mrs. Harding said, handing something to Sam. "I put this in the car, in case we needed it." Sam held it up, grinning. It was a leather halter with a brass nameplate reading APRIL MORNING—SAM HARDING.

"I worried I'd never get to use this," Sam said. She gave Stevie her halter back and led April into Max's trailer.

In a moment Sam, her parents, Max, and Judy were all gone. The Saddle Club stood alone in the suddenly quiet driveway, Lisa still clutching Calypso's lead. Even Janey and Nickel had vanished.

"Well," Carole said, looking down at the money in her hand, "I don't know about you guys, but after that I could certainly use an ice cream."

"Let me put Calypso away," Lisa said.

"I'll go ask Janey if she wants to come," Stevie said. "You guys should have seen her galloping bareback. She's amazing! I'm going to miss her when she goes home."

* * *

JANEY WAS BRUSHING Nickel's forelock. The pony was already cooled and snug in his stall, and just outside the door Stevie saw a bucket covered with a towel. "Red said I could give Nickel a hot bran mash," Janey explained. "I just mixed it, so it's not ready yet."

"Do you want to go get some ice cream?" Stevie asked.

"No, thanks." Janey smiled. "My mom's going to pick me up pretty soon. We have to go into the city and meet my dad, and Mom's going to be mad enough when she sees how dirty I am. I was supposed to try to stay clean today. So she'd better not have to come looking for me, too, or I'll really catch it."

"Some other time," Stevie promised. "We eat a lot of ice cream in this country." She started to walk back to where Lisa and Carole were waiting.

"Stevie!" Janey called.

"Yes?"

"Wasn't that gate smashing?"

Stevie grinned at the enthusiasm in Janey's voice. "This whole afternoon," she answered, "has been smashing."

13

At TD's, THE ice cream parlor just down the road from Pine Hollow, The Saddle Club slumped into their favorite booth with shared expressions of relief. "Being a knight on a bay horse," said Stevie, "is tiring."

"So is being a media celebrity," said Lisa.

Carole laughed. "So is being a regular person," she said, "because that's what we are."

Their usual waitress came up to the table. Instead of giving them her usual scowl, however, she smiled. "I caught your show today," she said. "Nice work."

"You listen to the radio?" asked Lisa. Somehow she'd never thought of the waitress as doing anything but waitressing.

"Of course," the waitress. "And listen, I told the manager here what you kids did, and he says your sundaes are on the house. The only catch is"—she winked at Stevie—"they gotta be normal sundaes. Stuff regular human beings would eat." Stevie was known for ordering sundaes that only Stevie would eat.

"Thanks!" Lisa said, a little amazed by the offer but willing to accept a free sundae nonetheless. "I'll take hot butterscotch on vanilla ice cream."

"I'd like marshmallow topping on chocolate," said Carole. "And a big glass of water."

Stevie looked agonized. "I'll have crème de menthe topping . . . ," she said. She paused.

"What kind of ice cream?" the waitress prompted her. "Vanilla? Chocolate chip?"

"Peanut butter," mumbled Stevie.

The waitress snapped her order pad shut. "That's not free," she said. "That is not a normal sundae." She walked away.

"I couldn't help it!" Stevie said in response to her friends' laughter. "It was the only thing that sounded good to me. It doesn't matter if it's not free—we've got the money from Sam and April."

"Yeah," said Lisa. "I have to tell you, we've had a lot of Saddle Club projects. Some have been better, and some have been worse, but *Horse Talk* was definitely the weirdest. I can't believe how it all worked out."

"It was pretty disgusting there for a while," Carole agreed. "Last week, I figured it was just about the worst Saddle Club project on record. Now that we've found

131

April—well, if it weren't for all the bad stuff in the first three weeks, this would have been one of the best projects."

"I'm going to kill Chad," Stevie muttered.

"Yeah," said Lisa, "but you know, the first week wasn't great either, when no one called in."

"It's amazing how many people were listening to today's show," said Carole. "I guess we have to consider *Horse Talk* a success."

"They were just listening to hear themselves make stupid jokes at our expense," Lisa argued. "I'm not sure that counts as a success."

"But as soon as things got serious, they quit calling in with jokes," Carole pointed out. "You were really great on the air, but the callers were paying attention, too."

"Typical Chad," Stevie said. "He didn't mind making fun of us—I mean, really making fun of us—and he didn't mind getting all his friends to make fun of us, too. But he does know enough to quit joking when he needs to. A missing pregnant horse is no joke. Even slimeballs like my brother understand that."

"And you even understand slimeballs like your brother," Lisa said, teasing her. "It's amazing."

Stevie shook her head. "Funny, isn't it? When you consider how little I understood Janey. At first, I mean. She's a terrific kid. I guess in the beginning we just didn't understand each other's background."

Lisa and Carole grinned at each other. "I think that at first you didn't realize Janey *had* a background," Lisa said. "As soon as you started listening to what she had to say, you started liking her."

"I agree," Carole said. "But you're not the only person who wasn't listening well this month. Think how close Lisa and I came to ignoring Missa! We almost didn't realize she was serious." She grinned. "Remember the bad lesson I had, before *Horse Talk*? Max said I wasn't listening to Starlight then, either."

Lisa used her fork to make prick marks on her placemat. "I guess we all learned a lot about listening this month. More than I would have thought."

The waitress appeared with their three sundaes. Setting them down in front of The Saddle Club, she announced, "They're all three on the house. The manager and I decided that peanut butter and crème de menthe is pretty tame for *you*." This last was directed at Stevie.

"I know," Stevie said. "I really wanted shredded coconut, too."

"Then you should have said so," the waitress declared. She walked away.

"Really, Stevie!" Lisa scolded. "Why didn't you say what you wanted? You might have learned a lot about listening, but now you need to learn to talk!"

Carole laughed. "I never thought I'd hear anyone say that to Stevie Lake!"

133

Stevie rolled her eyes at them and lifted a giant spoonful of ice cream to her lips. She swallowed the bite before speaking. "I'll work on it," she promised. "Tomorrow morning, I'm going to have a little chat with Chad."

ABOUT THE AUTHOR

BONNIE BRYANT is the author of many books for young readers, including novelizations of movie hits such as *Teenage Mutant Ninja Turtles* and *Honey, I Blew Up the Kid*, written under her married name, B. B. Hiller.

Ms. Bryant began writing The Saddle Club in 1986. Although she had done some riding before that, she intensified her studies then and found herself learning right along with her characters Stevie, Carole, and Lisa. She claims that they are all much better riders than she is.

Ms. Bryant was born and raised in New York City. She still lives there, in Greenwich Village, with her two sons.

Don't miss Bonnie Bryant's next exciting Saddle
Club Adventure . . .

HOLIDAY HORSE
The Saddle Club #72

It's New Year's Eve, and The Saddle Club is baby-
sitting so that Max and Deborah Regnery can have a
night off. Lisa, Carole, and Stevie think it will be a
peaceful evening, full of Monopoly, New Year's reso-
lutions, and talking past midnight. They didn't count
on seven-month-old Maxi. She's cute. She's adorable.
But she isn't ready to go to bed. The three girls have
to forget their plans and spend the evening trying to
tire Maxi out. But when a late-night phone call sends
them to the aid of a neighboring stable's horses, they
have a new problem: What should they do with
Maxi? Looks like she's about to get her first riding
lesson from The Saddle Club!